ON WINDS OF CHANGE

Copyright 2012 by Sharon Middleton

Thanks to:

Jesus, my Lord and Savior! His Spirit and Word prompted every word.

My husband, Michael, for his help in editing and his inspiration to keep going.

All my friends and family who had a hand in editing.

Foreword

Forgiveness is never easy. When a wounding blow is struck against ones-self or a loved one, forgiveness is far from our minds. Instead, our emotions and thoughts slide easily towards bitterness and revenge. Our consciousness is saturated with a sense of betrayal and a desire to retaliate.

As humans, we have a difficult time understanding the forgiveness of God. Jesus endured the ultimate measure of slander and betrayal on our behalf. He was totally innocent; totally unworthy of the slander and abuse, both physical and emotional. Yet, He forgave freely… even initiating that forgiveness before it was asked for when He cried "Father, forgive them… for they know not what they do ! " (Luke 23:34)

In writing "On Winds Of Change", I have hoped to shed a measure of light on the miracles of redemption and forgiveness. If we first contemplate the wonders of God's forgiveness, we will find forgiving others much more difficult to resist… and God will be much more able to use us as agents of redemption. By embracing the profound depths of forgiveness and redemption, we will be empowered to boldly invade the dark places of this world and to draw prisoners of darkness into the light.

Sharon Middleton

Beyond The Dark

Wound heart,
be thou set free;
wounded spirit,
fall to thy knee.
Look up! Look up!
Above the veil…
fix thy gaze beyond the gale.
Press through the storm,
the bitter night;
see with thy heart the dawn's fair light.
Beyond the dark,
there, waits the day.
Beyond the doubt, He lights the way.
Look up! Look up!
Above the veil…
fix thy gaze beyond the gale.

Michael M. Middleton
*from *Sacred Journeys*

CHAPTER 1

REFLECTIONS

"Please open your Bibles to the book of Matthew, the 26th chapter," Reverend Dale Cochran waited for the rustling of pages to cease. "We will be discussing the story of Mary and her anointing of Jesus' feet."

As the Reverend continued by reading the scripture, Bethany Salister drifted into a daydream. She was remembering back to when Jesus first became real to her.

✧✧✧✧

Bethany was fifteen and sitting in church with her parents, Bud and Martha. The day was sultry and most of the congregation's attention was elsewhere. Bethany's attention, however, was glued to the front of the church. Reverend Cochran was preaching about Jesus' crucifixion.

"He was dragged into the courtyard, tied to a pole and whipped until His flesh was torn to shreds. When I speak of whipped, I don't mean the ordinary leather straps we have now. These whips were leather straps with pieces of sharp, jagged metal tied to the striking ends."

Bethany pictured in her mind what might have happened to Jesus that day and she cringed.

"When they were finished, a robe of deep purple was placed on His shoulders and a crown of thorns was thrust upon His head. Then the soldiers came and mocked Him, struck Him in the face and spat on Him."

"Why was He treated so badly if all He was doing was telling people how to go to Heaven?" Bethany blurted out.

Chuckles could be heard around the room and Reverend Cochran smiled warmly.

"He needed to do what God had been telling the Jews for centuries. It's called fulfilling a prophecy."

"What happened next?" Bethany asked.

"When they were done, they took Jesus outside and made Him carry a very large beam on His back uphill on this road now called Via Del Arosa, which means 'Way of the Cross'. This beam was to be part of the cross on which He was crucified. When He reached the top of the hill, they laid Him on His back on the cross. Then they stripped Him of His clothing and nailed his feet and wrists to the beams. These weren't the small nails like we would use to build fences. These were nails the size of railroad spikes."

Some gasped with surprise and some hung their heads as the Reverend's description became real. Bethany's mind was flying!

"When the nails were secure, they hoisted the cross so it stood straight up. He wasn't alone, though. He was hung between two thieves. One thief had a mocking spirit, but the other asked Jesus if He could remember Him when he entered the Kingdom."
"When all was said and done and Jesus breathed His last breath, the sky went black and the earth shook. Mary, his mother, Mary Magdalene, and a few of the disciples and his brothers mourned when He was brought down and laid to rest."

Bethany thought how awful it must have been to watch Jesus die like a common criminal. She couldn't keep back the tears. The church was silent as Reverend Cochran closed with his final words.

"Jesus was buried in a borrowed tomb and three days later he rose from the dead…..Next week we will talk of the resurrection and its significance in our lives. Mrs. Petree, may we have our last hymn….."

Bethany never forgot what Jesus did for her and as a result, she prayed that same day to ask Jesus to be her Savior.

✧ ✧ ✧ ✧

Bethany became melancholy. It seemed the older she became the less real Jesus was to her. Part of the blame rested with her constantly dwelling on her singleness. Sighing, she returned her attention to the front of the church. Reverend Cochran was praying for the tithes and offerings.

Bethany slipped out of her seat unnoticed. She didn't feel like facing the good Reverend today; for he always met his congregation at the door following the service. She just needed to have some time alone to sort out her mixed emotions and confusing thoughts.

Exiting, she stopped at the bottom step of the church porch, closed her eyes and breathed the fresh sea air.

I'll take a picnic lunch to the Landing, she thought as she hopped in her wagon and drove off towards the north end of town.

CHAPTER 2

PFEIFFER'S LANDING

Pfeiffer's Landing was located near a small cove on the Pacific coast of the recently birthed state of Oregon. It had a population of almost 300 and most of them attended the Community Church at the south end of town. The few businesses were central and most of the residents operated small family farms in the neighboring countryside. In addition to meeting their own basic needs of sustenance, they grew cash crops of produce and coastal hay. A few families kept small flocks of sheep, from which they gathered wool which was spun to produce clothing and blankets for the local marketplace and for sale to logging companies which would frequently supply here on their way inland.

An old legend gave the town its name. Near the closing of the eighteenth century, a lone fisherman went adrift while sleeping on his boat one sultry evening. Through the night, he drifted up the coastline with the prevailing current. When he awoke, he had run aground on the beach. His name was Michael Pfeiffer. He had no interest in returning home for he had no family left and his fishing and fur trading endeavors were just barely able to put food on his table. So, he staked a claim on a piece of land close to the sea and called it 'Pfeiffer's Landing'. He married and began a family.

Over the years, people passing through decided to stay. That is how Pfeiffer's Landing grew as a town. When Pfeiffer passed away fifty years ago, his wife, Gladys, decided to donate their land to the town as a park. They called it 'The Landing'. Gladys Pfeiffer loved to sit on her back porch and watch people relaxing and playing on the beach not too far down the trail. When she passed away a few years later, her children left the house to the town as a museum. It still stands today and the park is one of Bethany's favorite spots to get away; to relax and to think.

Bethany, now thirty years old, lived in the house she grew up in, on the northern end of town. Her parents were gone and had left the farmhouse and a small inheritance to her. She was an only child.

The Lord had not seen fit to give her a husband so she lived alone. Most of the women her age were married and raising children so she really had no one to talk to; except herself, her plants, occasionally Bessy (the family cow) and the Lord…of course. Oh, and her best friend, Sadie, who lived up the road a piece.

The beach park was only a quarter of a mile from her house so Bethany traveled there often. She loved the beach. The wide-open expanse of the ocean and the peaceful music of nature always reminded her of the Lord.

She was excited about her day at the Landing. She didn't want to run the wagon too hard for it was rather old and in very poor condition.

"I need to sell this old thing," she sighed to no one in particular.

When she reached the Landing, she tied the horses and nearly ran for the beach. She spread a blanket, set her picnic basket down and stood and looked around. No one was there, which was a rarity. She was glad about that. She wanted to be alone with her thoughts…and with God.

The sky was a clear blue with the sun shining bright and warm. The sea was calm and the tide was out. To her left was a wonderful rock formation that was shaped like a wolf howling at the moon and about a quarter mile of tide-pools. To the right was beach as far as you could see. A light-house stood about two miles distant. Just behind Bethany's right shoulder was a trail leading into the small grove of cedars that sheltered the museum from the wind. Bethany loved this place. She felt so close to God here.

Closeness to God had been rare these days for Bethany. She had been so distracted. She struggled with pride and loneliness often. However, her biggest problem was impatience. She was tired of being alone with nothing to do to keep her busy but the daily chores and an occasional craft.

She sat on the blanket, closed her eyes, emptied her mind and just listened. A cool breeze blew her auburn hair from her face. Sea Gulls chattered for food and the ever present melody of the waves resounded in the crisp afternoon. Then she heard it; a voice. She was startled at first and looked around to see if anyone was there. No one was there. She closed her eyes again and waited.

"***Rest***", the voice whispered long and slow.

Bethany definitely heard it that time. She jumped up and looked around, but she saw no one. That's all Bethany needed; the added stress of someone watching her. Then she thought about it. The voice said 'Rest'. Could it be God speaking?

"Lord, I've been 'resting' my whole life. Give me direction." Bethany was now kneeling on the sand in front of her blanket. She remained there for several minutes, but no other words came. She opened her basket. She wasn't very hungry, but she felt the act of eating would take her mind off things. As she bit into a piece of fried chicken, she heard rustling in the bushes behind her.

"Good afternoon," a stranger bellowed.

"Hello," Bethany said guardedly.

The stranger was rather tall. He had a few day's growth of beard and his clothes were slightly tattered and in need of a good laundering. His eyes were a startling clear blue; like the ocean in some far away tropical place.

"My name is Seth Gates. Could you please tell me when the museum is open?" He gestured with one hand and a slight tilt of his head as he asked.

"Um…It won't be open until ten… tomorrow morning." Distracted by the stranger's haunting eyes, Bethany had lost all hint of appetite and began busying herself by putting the food away.

"Hmmm…Do you know where I could find a place to rent a room?" Seth looked tired, but his ocean blue eyes sparkled.

Suddenly aware that her mouth was slightly agape, Bethany shook herself from the melancholy trance and replied, "Um…There's Mrs. Petree's Boarding House in town. Go south on that trail there. Mrs. Petree's is the first building on the right as you enter town." She pointed the way and started shaking out her blanket.

"You don't have to leave on my account," the stranger said, a little embarrassed. "It's just that you're the first person I've seen in three days. I've been traveling through the foothills north of here." Seth looked out over the ocean, closed his eyes and breathed in the fresh sea air.

Bethany watched him and smiled. Seth Gates looked like he could use rest, a bath and food. She thought for a moment.

"Would you like to join me…for some fried chicken?" she asked, spreading the blanket out again. "You look like you haven't eaten in a while." She smiled at him.

"Oh, I don't want to impose. I'll just…" he was turning to leave.

"You wouldn't be imposing. Truth is, I'm not very hungry and I was about to waste all this good food on the sea gulls. Please…come and sit." Bethany started pulling food out of the basket.

"Well, if you don't mind." He sat on the outer corner of the blanket. "Thank you, Miss…"

"Oh, please excuse me. My name is Bethany Salister. I was so startled by your approach that I forgot my manners. Pleased to meet you, Mr. Gates," she said, nodding slightly.

"I didn't mean to startle you. I saw you from a distance and it looked like you were busy so I didn't want to intrude." Seth was trying to eat like a gentleman, but it was very difficult. Bethany was right. He hadn't eaten in two days and was aching from hunger.

"Oh, I was just complaining to the Lord as usual. I can do that anytime." She watched Seth as he ate. She could tell that she was right about this stranger needing food. "Um...May I ask you a question?"

"Sure," he said, averting her gaze.

"When was the last time you ate?" She felt sorry for him.

Staring out to sea, he said, "Two days ago. That's when the last of my rations ran out and I lost my hunting knife so..." he seemed embarrassed, but very honest.

"Well, Mrs. Petree will take good care of you. She has a soft spot in her heart for people of consequence." Bethany faced the sea and just breathed in the sea air. Seth watched her with curiosity.

"Um...May I ask *you* a question, Miss Salister?" he asked rather hesitantly.

"Certainly," she replied, still facing the sea.

"Why were you complaining to the Lord? I mean...God gave us life and created everything around us. I don't see what there is to complain about." He blushed at his forwardness. "Forgive me. I get a little preachy sometimes."

"That's okay. You're right. There really isn't anything to complain about." Bethany's expression became clouded. "I'm just a little impatient with what God's plan is for my life. I have no family left so I'm alone. I just want to do something with my life; something that will make a difference." She kicked the sand for emphasis. She suddenly wondered why she had revealed her secrets to a total stranger.

"But ...you didn't come to hear me whine. Finish all you want from that basket. I'm going to walk down to the tide pools. If you don't mind waiting, I'll give you a ride into town." She stood and brushed off her skirt.

"You don't have to do that. I'll just walk. Thank you just the same." He sat staring out to sea.

"It's no trouble...really. Just relax and I'll be back in a few minutes." She started walking down the beach to the tide pools.

Seth watched her go. *She's a beautiful, seemingly intelligent young lady,* he thought. *Lord, why have you brought me to this town? Is Miss Salister the reason or am I just passing through again?* Seth prayed in frustration. He could understand how Bethany felt. He had felt that way for the whole year he'd been on the road.

"Are you ready?" Bethany broke his thoughts.

"Yes, thank you." Seth helped Bethany put the basket and blanket in her wagon.

"Do you have any belongings?" she asked.

"Oh, I almost forgot." He pulled a carpet bag and small bedroll from the bushes and set them in the wagon. "Thank you for your help, Miss Salister. I really appreciate it," he said as he climbed in.

"My pleasure, Mr. Gates," and she flicked the reigns to bring the horses to life. As they rode, Bethany did not want to ignore the refreshing feeling that had come over her since the arrival of this interesting stranger. Maybe the Lord was listening after all.

CHAPTER 3

MRS. PETREE

Ingrid Petree was of Swiss descent and had lived in Pfeiffer's Landing most of her life. Her parents had built the boarding house when she was but two years old. At that time, Mrs. Pfeiffer was still alive. Ingrid loved to visit her and play on the beach, which extended inland nearly to the Pfeifer's back door.

Fifty years later, Ingrid was running her boarding house alone and loving it. Occasionally, she wondered what it would have been like to have a family of her own. Her husband, George, died young of an illness that had plagued him most of his life. They never had any children. There were a few times when she came close to marrying again, but no one could hold a candle to her George. All-in-all, she was happy with life in its present state of being.

Ingrid was in the kitchen preparing supper when she heard the front door bell. Its cheerful jingling shook her from her reminiscing and alerted her that someone had entered. Wiping her hands on her crisp, sunny-yellow apron, she walked out to greet her guest.

"Well, hello, Bethany," she said in her sweet, soft voice.

"Hello, Mrs. Petree. This gentleman would like a room." She pointed to Seth as he paced somewhat noisily across the wooden floor to the front desk.

"Hello, young man. I am Mrs. Petree and I am the proprietor here. We do not have any boarders right now so you may take your pick of any of our fine rooms." She opened the guest ledger. "May I have your name?"

"Seth, ma'am… Seth Gates. I've been traveling for the last three days through the foothills and would just like a bath and a bed." He pulled out a faded, well-worn pocketbook in order to pay.

"How long will you be staying with us, Mr. Gates?" Mrs. Petree asked, adding his name to the ledger.

"I'm not right sure yet. I'd say no more than a week... How much is it?" he asked sheepishly.

"A dollar a day and that includes meals and maid service."

Seth looked dry-mouthed into his pocketbook. He had ten dollars left to his name. "Um...may I pay a day at a time? I don't have too much left... and I don't know how long I'm going to be here."

Bethany watched from the doorway. She wanted to make sure Seth was settled before she left. She glanced at Mrs. Petree and noticed she wasn't smiling anymore. She looked almost angry. Or, at least slightly less cordial than she'd seemed when this paying guest first approached the front desk.

"Certainly," Mrs. Petree said with strained politeness. "That will be fine, Mr. Gates. We will put you in room two on the second floor." She turned away in an attempt to conceal a growing dismissive tone. "It has a wonderful view of the ocean..." She said flatly, making the necessary adjustments in her ledger and handing him a rather old-fashion looking key. "Meals are at seven in the morning, twelve noon and six in the evening. Cleaning is done on Tuesdays and Thursdays."

"Thank you." Seth gave her a dollar, picked up his things and headed for the stairs. He paused, "Thank you for your help, Miss Salister. I appreciate it more than you know." Turning, he climbed the twelve steps leading to the second floor, turned, and paced down the narrow hall to his room.

"You're welcome!" Bethany called after him. She turned to leave, but Mrs. Petree called her back.

"Bethany, might I have a word with you?" She gestured, asking Bethany to follow her to the kitchen.

Bethany took a seat at the kitchen table while Mrs. Petree continued with supper preparations.

"Is something wrong, Mrs. Petree?" Bethany was a little concerned that she might have overstepped propriety.

"Oh, nothing is *wrong*, child. I was just going to ask you about Mr. Gates." Mrs. Petree deftly avoided looking at Bethany while she talked.

"What about him?" Bethany knew where this was leading. Mrs. Petree was very nice and tried to look after people in need when she could, but she was also very protective of Bethany. Perhaps too protective at times.

"Well, to state it directly…why was he with you?" Mrs. Petree still refused to look Bethany in the eye.

"I was out at the Landing and he asked where he could get a room. I was heading into town so I offered him a ride." Bethany blushed with frustration. "Did I do something wrong?" She took deep, slow breaths in order to regain her composure.

"Well, you know it is not proper for a lady to be alone with a man unless they are courting." Mrs. Petree couldn't believe a grown woman like Bethany would do such a thing.

Bethany said nothing. She stared at the floor trying to regain her confidence and composure before she spoke to Mrs. Petree. She didn't want to hurt her feelings.

"He could have done something to you or hurt you in some way." Mrs. Petree was genuinely concerned. "I am just concerned for your welfare, dear." Mrs. Petree had been protective of Bethany since her mother died. Mrs. Petree and Martha Salister were best friends since they were children.

"Mrs. Petree," Bethany paused as she silently counted to ten. "he seems like a very nice man and speaks like he knows the Lord. I mean no disrespect, but you should get to know someone before you judge them!" Bethany abruptly stood and started for the door.

"Bethany, wait… I did not mean to upset you, dear!" Mrs. Petree said, truly embarrassed. Bethany grabbed the door and swung it open with emphasis.

"Good day, Mrs. Petree!" Bethany bit off through clenched teeth. She slammed the screen door as she left.

"Is something wrong, ma'am?" Having returned downstairs, Seth had heard the whole conversation and felt sorry for Bethany.

Startled and somewhat embarrassed, Mrs. Petree shook her head and paced briskly back into the kitchen.

Seth walked out to the front porch and looked up and down the main road through town. He noticed Bethany's wagon heading toward the south end of town where he could see a mercantile sign. He sighed deeply. It was the same in every town he visited. Someone would offer to help him and some busybody would ruin his reputation before the first day had ended.

Lord, why can't people just accept me as I am? he prayed silently. *It's taxing my strength, Lord. Give me direction. What is my purpose in this town…? Your beauty is all around us here, Lord. Can't I stay and rest here a while?* Seth sighed once more and retreated back up the twelve steps to the cool, dimly lit hallway and into his room.

CHAPTER 4

LEADING AND FOLLOWING

Bethany was so upset at Mrs. Petree that she finished her shopping at Skinner's Mercantile in less than five minutes. Shopping was sort of a hobby of hers and it was rare that she would spend such a short time patronizing her favorite store. When she finished paying the clerk, she went straight home without a word to anyone. She hastily stowed away her purchases and strolled out back to sit in the porch swing. She spent a lot of time in that rickety old swing thinking and praying.

"Lord, I know Mrs. Petree means well, but why does she always have to be poking her nose in my life?" Bethany's farm was so far from town that she didn't mind praying out loud. "Forgive me, Lord, for being so rude to her. It's just so frustrating that nobody in this town sees me as an adult!" Her frustrations somewhat assuaged, her thoughts returned to that morning on the beach.

Bethany wondered what *'rest'* meant and remembered a scripture reference that might clarify. She rose and strolled thoughtfully inside to look for her Bible. Retrieving it from her reading desk, she flipped through the Old Testament. She found Habakkuk chapter two, verse three. Bethany read it aloud, *'For the vision is yet for an appointed time, but at the end it shall speak, and not lie: though it tarry, wait for it; because it will surely come, it will not tarry'*. She sighed deeply, "Okay, Lord," she whispered. "I'll try to be patient."

It was getting dark so Bethany fixed a sandwich, had a cup of tea, and went up to bed. However, sleep eluded her. All she could think about were those ocean blue eyes sparkling in the sunshine. She sighed and rolled over toward her window. She couldn't see anything outside for the moon hadn't risen yet, so she closed her eyes and tried to think of the rolling ocean waves. It usually helped her to relax and find rest. She was asleep before she could count to five.

✿ ✿ ✿ ✿

Back in his room, Seth suddenly craved a long, hot bath. He hadn't had one in more than a month and his muscles needed it nearly as much as his skin. He pulled back the curtain in the far corner of the room and noticed there was water in the bathtub already. It wasn't exactly hot, but it would have to do. He poured some bath salts in and undressed. The cool water was a shock to his system, but he got used to it quickly. It was better than ice cold mountain ponds and lakes. As Seth washed away the last few days of fatigue and dirt, he closed his eyes and played back the events of the day in his mind. He thought about the woman who helped him.

She's beautiful and intelligent, he thought as his muscles started to relax. *It also seemed she knew a lot about the Lord. I wonder if there's a church in town.*

Straightening up a bit, Seth opened his eyes and looked out the window to watch the sun disappear beneath the churning waves of the Pacific. Sunsets always reminded him of the Lord's power and grace.

"I'll walk the town tomorrow and see what I can find," he said as he climbed out of the tub, retrieving a towel neatly folded on a stool nearby.

He dressed for bed, unpacked, and climbed under the covers. He was asleep before his head came fully to rest upon his pillow. Although he didn't remember his dreams very often, the ones he had this night were filled with the auburn curls and emerald green eyes of the woman he had met earlier that day. He slept through the night without a stir.

✿ ✿ ✿ ✿

Mrs. Petree finished the kitchen chores just after the sun went down for the night. She was troubled and confused about her altercation with Bethany earlier that day. She was also worried about the tenant she had acquired. She didn't know if this man was a criminal, or a lunatic, or just an ordinary man of God without a home. As she turned down the covers on her bed, she felt the need to pray.

"Father," she whispered, kneeling at her bedside. "protect us while this stranger is here. Help him to find what he is looking for quickly. And, Lord… help Bethany to understand that I am only looking out for her best interests. Amen." Mrs. Petree rose and put out the lamp next to her bed. Then she slipped under the covers and fell asleep.

CHAPTER 5

WALKABOUT

Monday dawned bright and clear. Seth was up with the roosters at dawn and was dressed and ready to head out by a quarter to seven. As he strode past the kitchen, he stumbled directly into Mrs. Petree.

"Oh!" he said, steadying himself. "Good morning, Mrs. Petree. I'm sorry, are you all right?"

"Yes," she replied, straightening her apron and smoothing her hair. "Would you like your breakfast now, Mr. Gates?"

"Yes, thank you. I'm starved." Seth sat down at the finely appointed dining room table and waited.

When Mrs. Petree had finished placing all of the food on the table, she sat in the end chair opposite him and folded her hands.

"Would you… like to ask the blessing, Mr. Gates?" she asked in a subdued tone.

"I'd be honored," he said, bowing his head.

After the blessing, they helped themselves to a feast. Seth and Mrs. Petree ate for the most part in silence. The meal was delicious, but Seth's mind was on the day ahead; not on the taste of the bacon or the biscuits. He finished quickly, downed two cups of coffee, and was rising from his chair when Mrs. Petree spoke. "Will you be in for lunch?"

"I'm not certain, ma'am. Let's say if I'm not here by a quarter to noon, I won't be here 'til supper." Seth cleared his dishes and set them on the kitchen counter. Heading for the front door, he turned and said, "Have a nice day, Mrs. Petree." Smiling politely, he nodded and left.

Mrs. Petree finished the remainder of her coffee and cleared the rest of the dishes. In no particular hurry to finish the kitchen chores, she walked out to the back porch and gazed out over the swelling green sea. *He seems like a nice young man,* she thought. *I wonder what his story is.* She remained there for a few moments before walking back inside to start the daily chores.

✡✡✡✡

Seth strode casually down the street toward the mercantile. Next to the boarding house was the telegraph office and directly across the street was the livery.

I need to get me a horse, he thought.

Down the alley to his left he could see more buildings. "This will take me a while," he whispered, continuing down the street. After the alley there was the saloon on the right and an abandoned building on the left. Along the way, he passed a few patrons. He tipped his hat to the ladies and said 'good day' to the men, but it didn't look like much of the town had awakened yet. What Seth didn't notice was that most of the people he had passed on the street were now watching him and wondering just who he was.

On down the street he went… passing several houses and the sheriff's office and finally reaching the mercantile on the right. He walked up to the door and noticed a sign that said it would open at eight. Seth pulled out his old pocket watch and realized that he was about ten minutes early. He passed the time reading the bulletins and advertisements tacked to the wall outside the front door. There was a very old and faded notice on making quilts and bandages for the civil war. He read about a lost dog, a wanted outlaw that vaguely looked familiar, and a schedule for the ladies' book club.

"Mornin'," a voice called.

Seth turned to see an older gentleman approaching with a pistol strapped to his hip. "Good morning," he replied with a smile.

"I'm Sheriff Ryan Drake." He held out his hand to Seth.

"Seth Gates," Seth replied, shaking the sheriff's hand.

"What can I do for you, Mr. Gates?" Sheriff Drake said, folding his hands casually behind his back.

"Oh, I'm just waiting for the mercantile to open." Seth was a little intimidated.

"You... new in town?" the sheriff asked, narrowing his eyes a bit.

"Yes. I just got in last night." Seth decided to put the sheriff at ease. "I'm staying at Mrs. Petree's until I find work."

The sheriff sighed and relaxed. "Welcome to Pfeiffer's Landing. If you have any questions... just drop in to see me." He nodded towards the office down the street and turned to leave.

"Actually...I do have one question." Seth remembered where he might have seen the outlaw posted on the bulletin board.

"Yes?" The sheriff turned again and waited patiently.

"How long has that poster been hanging there?" he asked, pointing to the outlaw.

"Oh...about a year," the sheriff replied, rubbing his chin thoughtfully. "Why do you ask?"

"Have you caught the man yet?" Seth asked intently.

Sheriff Drake just shook his head and wondered why this stranger was so interested in a criminal poster that was a year old.

"I think I may have seen him in my travels," Seth said, looking at the poster with renewed concentration.

Sheriff Drake started at this revelation. His hand reached for his pistol on impulse. "Where and when?" he asked with new interest.

"I've been up in the foothills for the last three days. When I set up camp the first night, a man rode up looking for some water. I offered him part of my meal, but he refused. He asked if he could have some coffee and I told him it wouldn't be any trouble. He sat on a log next to my fire, drank two cups of coffee without so much as a thank you, got on his horse and left. I noticed the next morning that my hunting knife was missing. It was in my saddle bag... laying behind the log where the man sat... so I figured he may have taken it." Seth tried to remember what the man was wearing and what kind of horse he rode.

"Do you remember which direction he went?" the sheriff asked, jotting things down on a notepad he always carried.

"Well...my camp was by a stream that had a washed out bridge on it. He went up the hill behind me and disappeared into the trees. When I packed up the next morning, I noticed a weather worn sign by the trail. The only word I could read on the sign was 'mine'." Seth prayed that this information would help the sheriff.

"Thank you, Mr. Gates." The sheriff turned to go again and then called back, "Will you be stayin' long?"

"I hope so," Seth called back.

"Could I come to you with more questions later if I have to?" The sheriff kept inching towards his office, glancing back over his shoulder as he went.

"Certainly," Seth replied, smiling.

Sheriff Drake ran to his office and a few minutes later came riding out of the alley with two men riding after him.

"I hope they find him," Seth whispered. He turned his gaze to the bulletin board once more and noticed a small piece of paper in the bottom right hand corner.

WANTED:
STRONG, ABLE-BODIED YOUNG MAN.
GOOD WITH AX AND HAMMER.
SMALL RANCH IN NEED OF REPAIR.
INQUIRE WITHIN!

Seth thought about it and wondered if the job was still available. He heard the bells tinkle as an elderly woman unlocked and swung open the door to the mercantile.

Skinner's Mercantile used to be the largest store in town, but after Henry Skinner's death the previous summer, Mary Skinner had decided it would be best if she moved the store to a smaller building. She was getting on in years and didn't have anyone to help at the store, so she condensed the stock to just the needed items for the area. She retained ownership of the old store building, hoping to rent it out or sell it in the future.

Seth walked in and smiled at Mrs. Skinner as he began looking around.

"Good morning!" she greeted cheerfully. "Can I help you find somethin'?"

"No thank you, ma'am. I'm just looking around." Seth continued down one isle, looking left and then right without really paying attention to what he was looking at.

"That's fine, young man. Let me know if you have any questions." Mrs. Skinner smiled and started sweeping behind the front counter.

Her frail voice and the sparkle in her eyes made Seth feel at home. He smiled at the thought. It had been a long time since Seth felt at home anywhere. The woman reminded Seth of his grandmother.

"Ma'am?" Seth began as he walked towards the front.

"Just call me Nanna. Everyone does," Mrs. Skinner said as she smiled.

"Okay...Nanna. There's an advertisement out on the wall for a ranch hand. Is the job still available?" Seth was hoping he could stay awhile, but to do that, he needed a job to raise some money. This looked like the perfect opportunity.

"Yes, it is," said Mrs. Skinner. "But... it's not just ranch work. It also involves stocking my shelves when orders and supplies come in. Maybe a few other things."

"Oh, it's for you that I would be working?" Seth asked, his mind racing.

"Of course." Mrs. Skinner paused, puzzled by his question. "Does that bother you, young man?"

"Oh, no!" Seth smiled widely. "In fact, I was just thinking how much you reminded me of my grandmother, Florence." Seth waited anxiously for her reply.

Mrs. Skinner giggled. "That's sweet of you, son." She blushed as she spoke. "The ranch hand job is a live-in. Do you mind?" she asked, quickly changing the subject.

"No." Seth was surprised, but thankful. "As a matter of fact, I just got in to town last night. I've been traveling on and off for the last year. I guess you could call me a drifter," Seth said, chuckling slightly.

"Good. I need two strong arms around the ranch to keep things going. I can do most of it, but the good Lord is telling me to slow down and take it easy." Mary Skinner did not like to be dependent on anyone. She was learning, though. "The store job is easy. You just drive me to work, empty the delivery wagon, and stock the shelves. We're open Monday through Saturday from eight in the mornin' to four in the afternoon."

Seth thought about it only a few seconds. He had a strong feeling that he was here in this town for a reason. "You have yourself a deal," he said, extending his hand.

"Hallelujah!" Mrs. Skinner bubbled over while shaking his hand. Her grip was much firmer than Seth would have expected for a woman of her stature. "Would you like to start now? The delivery came late last night and sits out back as we speak."

"Sure! Can I come back in about an hour so I can collect my things from the boarding house?" Seth asked.

"Certainly, but what do I call you, young man?" she asked.

"Oh, I'm sorry. My name is Seth Gates."

"Nice to meet you, Seth. Welcome to our community." Her smile made him feel warm inside.

"Thank you…Nanna." Seth returned her smile and departed to get his things.

As he was walking up the street to the boarding house, his heart soared. He actually felt like he had come home. He couldn't wait to start his new job. Seth was smiling from ear to ear when he walked in the front door to the boarding house.

Mrs. Petree looked up from the front desk and smiled. "Did you have a nice walk, Mr. Gates?" she asked, shuffling some papers.

"Yes, I did! Thank you for asking!" Seth smiled all the way up the stairs. He packed, made his bed and came down to pay his bill.

"Mrs. Petree, thank you for letting me stay here. I really enjoyed the comfort and the peace." Seth signed out in the ledger and turned with a nod.

Mrs. Petree's smile disappeared. "You are not staying?" she asked.

"I got a job and they want me to start immediately." Seth was almost out the door.

"Mr. Gates?" Mrs. Petree called.

"Yes?"

"God bless you in your new adventure," she said with a small smile.

"Thank you. God bless you, too, Mrs. Petree." And he was gone.

"The Lord giveth, and the Lord taketh away," she said as she returned the ledger to its place and ascended the stairs to clean Seth's room.

CHAPTER 6

EMERALDS AND GUNFIRE

Seth's first day of employment at the mercantile was a busy one. He unloaded the previous night's delivery, stocked shelves and display cases with the various sundries and trinkets, cleaned the store from top to bottom, and memorized price lists and inventory sheets. A few customers came in that Mrs. Skinner introduced him to, but most seemed aloof; almost like they felt they were better than him. Seth didn't mind. He had a good job working for a real nice lady and he liked it here. *They're just going to have to get to know me better*, he thought as he swept the aisles with a stiff-bristled broom.

He heard the metallic chiming of the front counter bell and noted with a glance over his shoulder that Mrs. Skinner was still in the back storeroom. When he paced toward the front of the store, he saw Bethany standing there, adjusting the tie strings of her bonnet.

"Hello, Miss Salister," he said, sidestepping behind the counter. "What can I do for you?"

"Well…, Mr. Gates! I see you've found employment already. Congratulations!" she said warmly.

"Thank you. I'm really excited… and grateful! I like this town, but I didn't know how I was going to stay without any money. I noticed the advertisement for this job and inquired about it just this morning. Nanna wanted me to start right away… so here I am. Isn't God wonderful in providing for our needs?"

"Did I hear the bell?" Mrs. Skinner said, coming out of the back room. "Oh, good day, Bethany."

"Hello, Mrs. Skinner. How are you today?" Bethany inquired with a warm smile. She loved Mrs. Skinner like family.

"Oh, I'm just fine, dear... Did you meet my new clerk?" she asked, patting Seth on the shoulder.

"Yes. We met yesterday." A sudden wave of shyness overtook her. "Mr. Gates seems to fit in with the store just perfectly."

Mrs. Skinner smiled broadly. "Yes, dear... it's so nice to have broad shoulders and a strong back to do the heavy lifting again." She winked at Bethany and feigned a whisper, "And he ain't bad to look at either..."

Seth was embarrassed, but happy about the ladies' conversation. He was glad that he was helping out Mrs. Skinner. He felt sure that he was where God wanted him to be at the moment and actually felt content and settled for the first time in a long time.

"Well, Seth, if you have things under control here, I need to run an emergency order to the telegraph office." Mrs. Skinner hung her apron on a black iron hook on the wall behind the counter and headed for the door.

"Go right ahead, Nanna. I'll take care of Miss Salister's order." Nodding his consent, Seth waved her on and returned his attentions once again to Bethany.

"Are you going to be staying at the boarding house, Mr. Gates?" Bethany asked.

"No. Nanna has offered room and board in exchange for ranch work. I'll be living in the bunkhouse out at her place, I suppose." Seth was smiling and his ocean blue eyes sparkled. His 'mood' was contagious.

Suddenly remembering the reason for her patronage, Bethany began, "Um...I came to pick up some supplies I ordered last week. I believe they came in last night, but hadn't been unloaded yet when I dropped in earlier." Bethany was smiling now and trying very hard not to stare at Seth's beautiful eyes.

"Well, you just let me know what supplies you're looking for and I'll load them in your wagon for you," Seth said, heading for the stock room.

Bethany followed. "A bundle of 2x4's and some pine siding, a bucket of nails, one gallon of whitewash… and two crates of cedar shake shingles." She hoped she had remembered everything.

"What are you building…if you don't mind me asking?" Seth asked, reaching for the order tablet.

"Pardon me?" She was brought back from her daydream.

"What are you building?" he asked again.

"Building?" she repeated hesitantly, not wanting Seth to know she hadn't been fully paying attention.

"That order sounds like building supplies. What are you going to use them for?"

"Oh…I need to fix up my chicken coop and refurbish my feed barn for my cow. It's nothing special." She found it hard to pay attention for Seth's eyes were captivating.

"You going to do all that by yourself?" he asked as he began to gather the supplies and carry them out to the bed of her wagon an armful at a time.

"Yes. Why do you ask?" She asked with a furrowed brow.

Bethany always became defensive when someone was "looking out" for her. She had spent a lot of years alone and was used to her independence. She never thought anyone believed she could take care of herself so it was hard for her to accept help from others.

Seth noticed the change in her tone and backed off a little. "Oh, I was just wondering if you needed some help," he offered somewhat meekly.

"No, no thank you," Bethany said smugly. "I can handle it just fine."

Seth noticed a little flicker of fire in her emerald-green eyes and realized he had perhaps overstepped his bounds.

"Okay," he said, finishing the loading of the wagon. "Let me know how it turns out."

"Why?" she asked, briskly signing the delivery form.

"Because, I'd love to see it," he whispered, holding her gaze for what seemed like eternity. "Have a nice day!" He smiled and briskly turned to go back inside, leaving her slightly flustered.

"Good job, my boy," Mrs. Skinner said slyly, patting him on the shoulder. She had just returned from the telegraph office. "She could really use the help, but she doesn't like to take it."

"What are you saying, Nanna?" Seth blushed.

"Oh, Bethany has been single and alone for a long time. It's high time she settled down; raised a family." Mrs. Skinner winked at Seth as she turned and started washing windows.

"I was just being friendly," Seth said as he watched Bethany close the back of her wagon and climb onboard, taking up the reigns and releasing the hand break. Mrs. Skinner's remarks made him think.

✿✿✿✿

Bethany watched Seth retreat into the store, feeling shaken. She had held her ground with him, but realized the moment those eyes of his held her gaze, her defenses were down. She hated feeling vulnerable. She thought about those eyes all the way home. The clarity displayed in them reminded her of something, but she couldn't think what. When she got home and stared at her wagon, she realized her foolishness in refusing Seth's help.

"How am I going to do this by myself?" She raised her hands to the sky, sighed in frustration, then rolled up her sleeves and started unloading.

✿✿✿✿

Seth walked outside with the broom and slop bucket. He swept the boardwalk in front of the store and stacked the fruits and vegetables neatly. He pulled the produce that seemed past its usefulness and pitched it into the slop bucket by the door. "Well, it'll feed the critters, anyway."

All of the sudden, he heard gunshots from up the street. He noticed a crowd beginning to gather outside of the saloon and glanced at his watch, perplexed. "What could be so life threatening at the saloon at three in the afternoon?" he thought aloud.

"Oh, it's probably just Zane Alan blowing off steam again," Mrs. Skinner huffed, walking back inside.

"Who's *Zane Alan*?" Seth asked, carrying the broom and slop bucket back inside. The name sounded familiar to him, but he couldn't place it.

"He's the proprietor of the saloon… and a real hothead," Mrs. Skinner said with a note of contempt. "If he's had too little sleep… too much drink… well, usually both… and someone even looks at him wrong, he yanks his pistol and blows a hole in something. Or someone."

"Sounds like he needs Jesus," Seth said, rubbing his chin and chuckling mildly.

"He roughed up the last person who tried to get him to darken the threshold of a church building. The only one he sort of respects is Reverend Cochran… and it ain't clear whether it's respect or just superstition." Mrs. Skinner was counting the receipts for the day while Seth locked the door and pulled the heavy drapes closed on the store windows.

"Sounds like a real challenge of a person to get to know," Seth said with a clever grin as he finished up the sweeping and stowed the broom in a corner behind the counter.

"Don't you be gettin' any ideas, Seth! Zane can be a real dangerous person. The best you can do for him is pray and stay out of his way." Mrs. Skinner locked the cashbox in the safe and hung up her apron on the back of the storeroom door. "Are you ready to go?" she asked, grabbing a small, neatly wrapped bundle of groceries.

"You bet!" he said, hanging up his own apron. "I'll fetch the wagon and be right back."

Mrs. Skinner ran out the back door after him. "Do you have all your things together?" she called.

"Yep. This carpet bag and bedroll's all I got." Seth helped her into the wagon, stored his things, and climbed in. "Which way?" he asked, grasping the reins in his dusty hands.

"South, my boy. Just head south out of town and I'll let you know when we're there." Mrs. Skinner sat back and prepared herself for an enjoyable ride home. She hadn't had anybody drive her anywhere since Henry's funeral the previous summer.

"You've got it!" Releasing the brake, Seth snapped the reins and off they went. He listened to Mrs. Skinner explain how the town was founded and how she came to own the mercantile and run it on her own.

In the back of Seth's mind, he thought of Zane Alan. He'd have to pray and see what the Lord wanted him to do. Surely, nobody was beyond redemption… he knew this all too well. Perhaps the Lord could reach Zane through the broken vessel he knew himself to be. But he was in no hurry to get a gut full of lead. He wouldn't be hasty in trying. "The better part of valor…" he mumbled to himself.

CHAPTER 7

THE BAR 'S'

They reached 'The Bar S' ranch in about thirty minutes at a leisurely pace. Seth enjoyed the ride out, with Mrs. Skinner pointing out special spots here and there. Nothing, however, prepared him for the scene he now witnessed as they pulled in the front gate.

He could tell that the ranch had once been the talk of the town. Now, though, he was wondering what he may have gotten himself into. The arch over the front entrance depicting the name of the ranch was falling down and missing letters. The fence and front gate were barely even there. All he could see were the posts and a few faded, weather-worn slats. He could already see that the outside of the ranch home needed some major repairs. He vainly hoped the interior would be in better shape. To the right of the house and behind about ten yards was the corral and a half-way caved in barn. To the right of that was the bunkhouse. His new home had no glass in the windows. There was a foot-sized hole in the door and the roof had weeds and grass growing on it. To the left of the ranch house was the chicken coop (which looked okay) and beyond that was a forgotten pasture.

"Well, Seth, this is the Bar 'S'; your new home. What do ya' think?" Mrs. Skinner beamed with pride.

"Um…it looks…lived in." Seth didn't quite know where to start.

"Well, let's go wash up for supper. I'll make some stew and biscuits while you unhitch the horses and send them out to pasture. You can put your things in the bunkhouse and I'll ring the dinner bell when it's ready." Mrs. Skinner grabbed her bundle and went inside to start supper.

"Lord, I need your strength," Seth whispered. "This place is falling apart." He unhitched the horses and sent them out as Mrs. Skinner had asked. He was reluctant to check out the bunkhouse, though. He picked up his things and took his time walking to his new home.

When he reached the door, he breathed a quiet 'help' and slowly stepped inside. He could tell the place had been deserted for some time. There was a layer of dust on everything in sight and cobwebs ruled the rafters.

The furniture was sparse, but looked as if it were in fair condition. Two sets of bunks were on the right wall. There was a stone fireplace with a kettle on the back wall, in the center. A table and six chairs were roughly in the middle of the one-room cabin and a small woodstove and washbasin were on the left wall. There was one medium-sized hole in each wall where windows used to be and two smaller vacancies adorned the front door.

Seth dropped his belongings on the table, raising a puff of dust, and walked over to the washbasin. After priming with water left in an old jar, He gave the water pump a good push. All that he received was air and a slight gurgling sound, followed by a pathetic whistling gasp of sorts. He pumped several more times and brownish water started to spurt out. He kept pumping until the water looked safe enough to drink and then stuck his head under the spout. He washed up, changed his shirt, and combed his hair. Then he heard the bell.

"Here goes nothing, Lord," he quipped as he walked up to the main house and entered for supper.

✰ ✰ ✰ ✰

A short time later, Seth and Mrs. Skinner were finishing up their meal.

"Ohhhh," Seth moaned, rubbing his belly. "I feel like a turkey on Thanksgiving." He pushed away his plate. "That was delicious, Nanna."

Seth looked around the dining parlor. There were many old photographs on the wall opposite him. "Who are all these people?" he asked as he studied each one intently. He could see similarities in a few.

"Thank you, Seth," she said, clearing the dishes.

Mrs. Skinner brought out some coffee. "That's all I have left of my family history." She went on to name most of them: aunts, uncles, cousins, children. Her hand rested on a picture of a handsome, young gentlemen dressed in a suit. Seth could see one single tear glistening on her cheek.

"This is my husband, Henry," she sniffed. "He passed on last summer. He'd been fighting influenza for months and his poor body couldn't hold out any longer. I miss him most at night. We used to read the Bible before we turned in for the night." Mrs. Skinner turned and poured two cups of coffee then sat down.

Seth waited while Mrs. Skinner composed herself.

"We had two children, a boy and a girl," she continued, pointing to their pictures. "Our girl, Angelina, was killed when she was thrown from her horse. She landed on a sharp rock that pierced her skull. And our boy, Joshua, was killed in the battle of Gettysburg. Neither one of them had married yet so I have no family left."

"I'm sorry, Nanna. I didn't mean to pry into painful memories." Seth's heart ached for what this woman had been through.

"That's all right. I'm not alone anymore," she said, grinning and patting Seth's hand.

"That's right!" Seth finished his coffee and pushed back his chair. "What time do we leave in the morning?" he asked as he rose to leave.

"We'll go in early and close by three so we can come home and you can get acquainted with the ranch and start some repairs. All the tools and supplies are in the shed right outside the back door." She pointed to the kitchen door.

"Okay. Where would I find cleaning supplies and fresh linens? I'm going to restore the bunkhouse to some sort of order before I go to sleep." Seth had his second wind now and felt he could clean the whole bunkhouse tonight.

"Linens are in the cedar chest in the hall and cleanin' supplies are in the cabinet by the back door. Oh, and the broom is right next to the stove... in the kitchen." Mrs. Skinner cleared the coffee cups and helped Seth get out all the supplies he needed.

"Thank you, Nanna. I'll see you in the morning for breakfast." He was walking out the front door.

"Good night, Seth." She shut the door when Seth reached the bunkhouse.

Seth saw her lamp in the front hall go out about ten minutes later. "Lord, I feel I have a purpose in this town now. I finally feel like I belong somewhere. Bless Nanna and give her peace in her heart about her husband and family. Lord, let her know she's never alone. Bless Miss Salister and help her to see to the other side of her problems. And, Lord...show me how you want me to approach Zane Alan. From first impressions, he's angry and maybe bitter over something that happened in a church somewhere. How do I talk to him..." Seth chuckled. "without getting shot?"

Seth said his 'amens' and began the arduous and long-neglected task of cleaning the bunkhouse. He wasn't fully satisfied, but finally called it "good enough" at about one in the morning and fell into a well deserved slumber.

CHAPTER 8

LEARNING TO TRUST

Bethany woke up Tuesday morning sore, but satisfied. She had managed to unload all of the building supplies she had purchased the previous day and performed some basic preparations for the task ahead, including cutting some of the framing boards to length. Not long after the sun had gone to bed, she covered the supplies with an old oiled canvas tarp to protect them from the morning mists. She then followed the sun's example and retired for the evening.

Now fully refreshed after a peaceful night's slumber, she gazed out her bedroom window toward the graceful willow swaying in the morning breeze. She loved that noble old tree in the backyard. She used to climb it when she was young. She would climb as high as she could and just sit and listen to the sound of nature: wind, rain, birds of all breeds and varieties. And, of course, there was the ever-present voice of the sea in the distance. This she treasured above all other songs. To her, no other voice in all of creation spoke more deeply of peace or serenity than the eternal song of the mighty Pacific.

This morning, she listened dreamily to the leaves of the willow rustling in the breeze. When Bethany was quiet in spirit, she noticed that nature had its own unique music. It relaxed her... and spoke wisdom to her heart in ways which simply could not be phrased in terms of human speech.

Bethany knew, though, if she didn't get out of bed soon, nothing would get done. She stretched and slowly sat up, noting the achiness of her muscles. The cool sheets were difficult to abandon, but the day would not halt its progress on her account. Draping her robe around her shoulders, she shuffled down the stairs to start some coffee and prepare something to eat. Her mind was racing with all the things that needed to get done before supper. *Cast your cares*, she thought, with a slight note of good-humored sarcasm.

When she had finished eating and the kitchen chores were done, she dressed and went out to collect eggs from the chicken coop. She kept only three hens and the obligatory rooster, but it was sufficient for her. Too many other families in the area kept their own coops for it to be worth the effort of trying to sell any surplus. What she gathered beyond her own needs, she would pass along to Reverend Cochran or Mrs. Skinner.

"Hello!" someone called in the distance.

"I'm back here, Sadie!" Bethany replied, cupping one hand around her mouth. There was no mistaking the voice of her neighbor, Sadie Alan.

"Hi, Beth. How are you?" Sadie called out, pacing around the corner of the house. She always seemed so cheerful. Sometimes Bethany allowed herself to be irritated by that. How could someone always be happy, even in the face of trial and change? Some people just didn't have the sense to know when to be distressed…

"Howdy, Sadie! I'm doing well… a little sore, but well enough. What's new in your life?" Bethany continued plucking eggs from the hens' nests, placing them gingerly in her woven straw basket.

"Oh… nothing really. I just came over to see if you needed a hand with your project. Zane never came home last night and I didn't want to be in his sights when he does stumble in." Sadie allowed a moment of resigned sadness to flash across her face. Zane was her older brother and the only family Sadie had left. She was afraid that someday he'd come home in a pine box, instead of a drunken stupor.

"I am so glad you thought of me," Bethany sighed in a brighter tone. "Sometimes my pride gets in the way of making sound decisions. I refused help yesterday and today my muscles are informing me of their disapproval!" Bethany walked the eggs inside, placing them in her icebox. "Would you like something to drink, Sadie? I have some fresh lemonade. Or perhaps a sarsaparilla?"

"Maybe later," Sadie replied, "So, what is this big project of yours, anyway?"

"Oh, I'm just fixing up my coop out there," Bethany said, pointing in frustration. "That old thing is about to fall to pieces… and I was thinking of adding a few more hens. The good reverend always seems so happy when I drop some eggs by…"

"You don't seem too happy about the idea," Sadie said, trying to get Bethany to open up to her.

"Which idea; the 'fixing up' or adding the hens?" Bethany grinned.

"The building!" Sadie replied, playfully slapping Bethany on the shoulder.

"Well, it just goes back to that pride thing." They both strolled out and sat on the back porch, procrastinating. "I get so angry at myself sometimes. I let pride control me so easily. Then I read in God's Word where it says, *'Better to be of a humble spirit with the lowly, than to divide the spoil with the proud'*. It makes me think sometimes that there is no hope for me." Bethany was clearly distressed about this, but Sadie was waiting for a prompting from the Lord before she replied. Sadie was deep in thought when she heard Bethany sigh.

"I'm probably boring you." Bethany stood up to walk back to the coop when Sadie spoke.

"You're not boring me! I was just thinking, that's all. I wanted to be sure that anything I said would be **His** words, and not my own." Sadie joined Bethany and helped her prepare the work area next to the coop. They uncovered the tools and supplies, folding the oiled canvas and setting it aside. They then began on the coop.

"And what did the Lord say?" Sarcasm dripped from Bethany's lips. Perhaps too much, she regretfully noted.

"Well, I recognize that scripture you mentioned. It's in Proverbs, right?" Bethany nodded. "Well, the verse right after that says, '*He who handleth a matter wisely shall find good: and whosoever trusteth in the Lord, happy is he*'."

"I seem to have a little problem trusting God right now." Bethany picked up the hammer and slammed a nail, bending it in half.

"Why?" asked Sadie, reaching for the next board Bethany had pointed at with the hammer.

"I don't know why. God has always provided for me in my hour of need." Bethany had nearly finished shoring up one whole side already and was surveying the second.

"What about the present? Does He provide for you now?" Sadie had picked up a second hammer and started on the side of the coop opposite Bethany.

"Well..." Bethany thought a few moments before answering. "I suppose He does. I mean, I have a roof over my head and food on my table, but..."

Sadie interrupted, "You're lonely?" She knew just how Bethany felt. She was lonely, too.

"I'm just so worried about my selfish needs, I don't see the provision." Bethany took her frustration out on another unfortunate nail.

"You told me of one when I first arrived here today," Sadie said, smiling.

"What's that?" Bethany was paying full attention to Sadie now, hammer forgotten.

"Me," Sadie said, pointing to herself.

Bethany threw the hammer to the ground and kicked the dirt. "You see? I didn't think of it because I was too busy complaining!" Bethany leaned against the fence, her energy spent for the moment. One lone tear made a slender trail in the dust on her cheek.

"It's okay, Beth. You shouldn't be so hard on yourself," Sadie said, putting her arm around Bethany's shoulders. "God forgives us if we just ask. Would you like me to pray for you?"

"Please?" Bethany was quietly weeping now as both she and Sadie bowed their heads to talk to God.

✡ ✡ ✡ ✡

Around four in the afternoon, Bethany put down her hammer. "Let's quit for the day. I'm tired, you look spent and I'm sure my stomach isn't the only one making noises."

"Okay. What shall we make for supper?" Sadie asked, following Bethany into the house.

"I don't know." Bethany thought a moment. "Do you want to stay here tonight? I have plenty of room."

"I don't want to impose," Sadie said, heading for the washbasin.

"Nonsense! You wouldn't be imposing. Tell you what…why don't you run home, pack some clothes and when you return, supper will be ready," Bethany said, washing her hands.

"Okay. I'll see you in an hour or so," Sadie said, crossing the front porch.

Bethany tramped upstairs to wash up and change into something more comfortable. She hated to admit it, but she had this pair of baggy trousers that used to belong to her father that she wore in the evenings sometimes. This day and age, she would be branded something awful if anyone ever saw her in them. She wasn't worried about Sadie, though. She had already seen Bethany in those old trousers. Sadie stayed with her often because her brother was quite aggressive and loud when he was drunk.

Bethany felt pity for Zane. He was always so angry and drunk. "I hope someone can open his eyes to the Truth," she whispered.

✡ ✡ ✡ ✡

Sadie returned sometime later with a change of clothes and a concerned expression on her face. Bethany noticed it the moment she walked through the front door.

"What's wrong, Sadie?" Bethany asked, concerned.

The look in Sadie's eyes answered for her. It was Zane again. "It's so hard to see my brother so angry and bitter!" she bit off. She slumped into one of the kitchen chairs and continued. "He came home while I was washing up. He just grabbed a biscuit, sat in Ma's rocker, and started screaming at me for no reason! I wish he would wise up and listen to someone tell him about the Lord. He needs a new attitude. His current one is going to get him killed." Sadie's voice trailed off into resigned frustration; she was spent of emotion for her brother. She loved him, but he had treated her so harshly for so long that she didn't care if he died right that minute.

Bethany could feel her pain; the pain of knowing that if Zane didn't shape up soon, he wouldn't go to Heaven. Bethany felt that same pain when her father died. Although he went to church every Sunday, he didn't know a thing about the salvation of Jesus Christ, and now Bethany feared she would never see him again.

"I have been praying for him, Sadie. I wish I could do more." Bethany patted her on the shoulder and brought supper to the table.

"You're doing far more than you think, Beth," she said, sadly. "You're a dear friend and you let me stay here when he gets like this. That means a lot," Sadie said, taking her first bite. "Mmm…Bethany, this is delicious!"

"Thank you. It was just something I threw together from the slop bucket," she said, laughing.

They both laughed now as they finished their tossed salad greens and hot bacon and cucumber sandwiches.

CHAPTER 9

SADIE AND ZANE

Sadie stayed with Bethany until Saturday. She enjoyed the company of a woman her own age. She never had any sisters, so she felt extremely blessed to have Bethany in her life. They had met and become friends soon after Bethany's mother died ten years before. They talked every waking moment the whole week.

On Saturday morning, Sadie paced down the stairs to the breakfast table looking rather melancholy.

"What's wrong, Sadie?" Bethany asked. "You look so down."

"Oh, I'm just thinking about my brother, again. I don't understand why he feels he needs to destroy his life and the lives of everyone around him." Sadie just picked at her food.

"Can I ask you something?" Bethany approached, hesitantly.

"Certainly," Sadie said, sipping her coffee.

"Why is Zane so angry? I mean…did something happen to him or someone he knows?" Bethany really wanted to know why Zane was the way he was. Every time she asked Sadie about this, Sadie would politely change the subject.

After a moment's hesitation, it seemed as if she was finally ready to let Bethany in on what was eating at her brother. "Well…about twelve years ago, he was working as a hotel clerk in our hometown. Florence is a little larger than Pfeiffer's Landing and has a busy port for shipments of all kinds. It's a pretty bustling little town." Sadie took a sip of coffee. "Zane was pretty happy then. I was still a teenager and thought he was a prince; that he could do no wrong." She was sounding a little sarcastic now.

"Are you okay talking about this?" Bethany asked. "You don't have to tell me..."

"It's okay." Sadie cut her short. "I've... I've never really told anyone except my parents, and they're gone now. I guess I can open up to a sister after all of these years. So... where was I?"

"You were still a teenager." Bethany smiled.

"Oh, yes." Sadie replied. Her expression took on a more somber tone as she continued. "Well, one day I was out in the pasture combing out Flash... Zane's stallion. He had just rolled in a patch of foxtail and was covered in them. It was a beautiful day; clear sky, warm sun, cool breeze. Zane was at work and Ma and Pop were napping. All of sudden, I heard footsteps coming up behind me and thought it was one of my parents coming to check on me. I didn't think to turn around. I just started talking. I said 'hello' and there was no answer. Before I could turn around, there was a hand over my mouth and another hand pulling me down to the ground. The man had a mask on so I didn't see his face...but I saw his curly blond hair and fierce eyes and knew immediately who it was." Sadie got up to refill her coffee cup. She stood at the stove with her back to Bethany.

"Did he..." Bethany was afraid to ask. "Did he...take advantage of you?"

"Yes..." Sadie said quietly. "Several times. He told me that if I made a sound, he'd kill me. He had a knife to my throat."

"Oh, Sadie," Bethany whispered. She was wide-eyed and nervous, waiting for Sadie to finish her story.

"When he finished," Sadie continued, trying to keep her composure. "He warned me not to scream or follow or tell anyone, or he'd kill me and my parents. I was frozen to the ground. I didn't move for what seemed like hours... except to cover myself with what shreds of clothing I had left." Sadie sat back down and stared into her cup. "When

Zane came home from work, he noticed Flash out in the middle of the pasture and he wouldn't come when Zane called for him. He walked out to see if maybe his reins were caught on something and found me all curled up on the ground, holding the reins and weeping like a baby."

"What did he do?" Bethany was breathless, wondering how much worse it could have been.

"At first he was so stunned that he just stood there. Then he asked me if I had fallen off the horse and maybe hurt myself, but all I could do was cry harder. Zane figured out what had happened by the looks of my clothes and started getting really angry. He yanked the reins from my hands, jumped on Flash and sped back to the house. In the next few minutes I heard my parents calling my name, so I slowly sat up so that they could see where I was. My father ran to my side and picked me up in his arms and carried me to my room. I told him to leave the room, so he set me on my bed and left, quietly shutting the door behind him." Sadie took a deep breath and folded her arms. She paused to catch her breath. "Zane never brought the subject up after that. He hardly talks to me about anything."

"It's a tragic story, Sadie. And pardon me for seeming insensitive by asking, but…why would that make Zane hate anything that has to do with church or God?" Bethany poured her cold coffee into the washbasin and sat down, waiting for Sadie's answer.

"The man was…the son of the pastor of the church we all attended."

Bethany gasped.

"He'd spent months trying to convince me to allow him to court me. I liked him as a friend, but that was all. He didn't want to accept that and I guess something inside of him just snapped." Sadie was staring out the window, void of expression.

"In time, I forgave him and told the pastor what had happened. He never believed me and…called me…a whore." Sadie cringed when she said the word. "The pastor and my parents got into an argument. In the end, the pastor banished us from the church, saying we were 'of the devil'. Everyone in town shunned us, so we had to move."

"Is that when you came to Pfeiffer's Landing?" Bethany asked.

"Yes…we moved here, just about ten years ago. I met you when I attended the 'Healing Shores Fellowship' for the first time, remember?" Sadie smiled at her friend. "My parents and brother never attended church again. My parents still had their faith, but Zane…he lost all trust in God and can't stand anyone associated with God. He vowed to my parents before they both died that he would take care of me, but…you know how that's been."

"It sounds like he blames it on you." Bethany shook her head in disbelief.

"I guess that's easier for him to believe. He loved God so much and his pet name for me was 'little lamb'." She stared at the table. "Now he figures no one will have me and he'll be stuck with me for the rest of his life. He is much older than me and has never been married…I'm just too much of an embarrassment to him, I guess."

"I don't think of you that way," Bethany said, patting Sadie's hand. "You're the best friend I've ever had. So you had something bad happen to you. You're still the same to me. More so even now that I know your past. I can't believe the joy that shines from you every time you talk about the Lord!" Bethany was smiling. "I can tell that the way you've endured this has made your faith stronger. It makes me feel special to know you and have you for a friend."

Sadie blushed and squeezed Bethany's hand.

They both rose to get dressed and went to collect the eggs for the day. They walked out to their newly finished coop and stood there staring at it for the longest time.

Bethany ran her hand along the side wall. "We did a pretty good job, didn't we?"

"We sure did! It's the prettiest chicken coop I've ever seen." Sadie opened the gate and walked inside. Bethany followed with a basket in hand. They collected the eggs and took them into the house.

"Hey, how about we take these eggs to town? I've been waiting on an order anyway," Bethany said, gathering her things.

"That sounds wonderful! I'll stop in and check on Zane's attitude… and probably go home with him." Sadie packed her things and walked outside to help Bethany hitch the horses to her wagon. "Hey, what should I do about Ima?" Sadie asked, worried about her horse.

"You can leave her here in my pasture and I'll bring her over to your house tonight." Bethany loved to ride Sadie's bay mare.

"Okay. Let's go," Sadie said with authority.

"Right. Let me shut the front door and you can get the gate on our way out." Bethany was excited now. She loved shopping in town. She snapped the reins and they were off.

CHAPTER 10

DE JA VU

Bethany and Sadie took their time getting to town. They talked all the way, enjoying the morning breeze from the sea. When they reached their destination, Bethany decided to leave her wagon and horses at the livery with the blacksmith, Bud Rafferty.

"Hey, Bud!" Bethany called.

"Howdy, Beth! What's new?" Bud asked, wiping his beefy hands on a rag.

"Nothing really. Could I leave these beasts with you and park my rig out front until I'm done shopping?" Bethany handed him the reins.

"Sure thing! I'll water 'em and give 'em a treat." Bud loved horses. He was especially fond of Bethany's two. They had once belonged to him.

"Thank you, Bud. I'll be back soon." Bethany waved as she and Sadie started down the boardwalk.

"Where do you want to go first?" Sadie asked excitedly.

Bethany was staring at Mrs. Petree's boarding house. "Um…I think I better stop at the boarding house first. I need to talk to Mrs. Petree."

"Okay. I'll walk down to Zane's. Meet me there when you're finished."

"Fine." Bethany waved goodbye and walked up the front porch of the boarding house.

She took a deep breath and walked inside. Mrs. Petree heard the bell and stepped out from the kitchen.

"Why, good day, Bethany! What…a surprise," she said, pretending to dust her front counter. "What can I do for you, dear?"

"Mrs. Petree…I need to apologize to you. I was really rude to you Sunday. I was wrong to treat you that way when you were showing concern for my welfare. I'm truly sorry," Bethany said, staring at the floor.

Mrs. Petree smiled. Her eyes were a little moist. Bethany had never treated her so respectfully before. "That's quite all right, dear. I realize you are a full grown woman and sometimes I forget that. I promise next time I will not be so nosy."

"Fine…well, Sadie is waiting for me so I'd better go." Bethany turned to leave and then turned back. "Have a nice day, Mrs. Petree."

Mrs. Petree was beaming with joy. "You too, dear," she said, and Bethany was gone.

✪✪✪✪

Sadie walked into the 'Silver Streak' saloon with one thing in mind: find Zane and get out quick. She hated the saloon. It felt like walking into the devil's lair.

The 'entertainment' was standing by the piano. Two young girls were listening to some random customer show off his meager musical talents and feigning awe at his exploits. As Sadie passed by, the girls glared at her coldly. They always thought Sadie might come to steal their prospects. Sadie was very beautiful. She had bright blond hair down to her waist that had a natural wave to it. Her eyes were hazel and as bright as the sun. She was petite and always wore a smile; except when she came to the saloon. The bar maids were not educated past the elementary basics so it was natural for them to be territorial. Territory was all they had in the world.

"Hello, Sadie," one of the girls cooed sarcastically.

"Hello," Sadie said, not stopping for a moment. She walked down the back hall to the office. She knocked once and walked in, not waiting for an answer. "Zane, can I ride home with you…" Sadie stopped in her tracks.

Zane was in his office chair with one of his girls sitting on his lap.

"Oh! Excuse me." Sadie walked out and was almost to the front door when Zane called for her to wait.

"Sadie, wait up!"

Sadie stopped at the front door, but refused to turn and face him.

"I'm sorry I yelled at you the other day. I was drunk… and stupid. Please come home?" he begged. But the only real reason he wanted her home was the cooking and cleaning. He held a strong aversion to both.

"Fine. What time do you want me to meet you?" she asked, her back still to him.

"Is four acceptable? Henry'll be taking over about then…" he asked in a controlled tone. He hated when his sister put on heirs.

"Fine." Sadie walked out and across the street to wait for Bethany.

✪✪✪✪

Bethany met Sadie across the street from the saloon. She could tell that Sadie was upset about something, but didn't wish to pry. "You want to go shopping at the mercantile? I have to bring these to Mrs. Skinner and then pick up my order, " Bethany asked, pointing to the egg basket on her arm.

"Sure," Sadie said, the brightness returning to her eyes. She took a deep breath and smiled.

They walked down to the mercantile and entered.

"Hello, Nanna," Bethany greeted. "I brought you some fresh eggs."

"Well, thank you, my dear," Mrs. Skinner said cheerfully. "What can I do for you young ladies?"

"I'm waiting on an order of fabric. Has it come in yet?" Bethany asked, looking around.

"I'm not sure. Seth's in charge of the orders now. Seth?" she called.

"Yes, Nanna?" Seth said, entering from the storeroom.

Sadie gasped and grabbed Bethany's arm. Then she ran outside.

"Sadie?" Bethany called, running after her.

Seth's face turned ashen. He hadn't seen that beautiful face in over ten years. He returned to the storeroom and sunk to the floor.

"Seth, what's wrong? You look like you've seen a ghost!" Mrs. Skinner was concerned. "Should I get Doc Brickner?"

"No," he breathed. "I---I'm okay."

Mrs. Skinner went back to the front. "Sadie?" she called outside.

"She's okay, Nanna," Bethany said. They were both sitting on the bench outside the store. "She just needed some air… I guess."

"Do you want me to get Doc Brickner, Sadie, dear?" Mrs. Skinner asked, brushing the hair from her eyes.

"No," she managed to say. "I…I'll be fine."

"All right." Mrs. Skinner turned to Bethany. "I'll check on your order."

"Thank you, Nanna," Bethany said, never taking her eyes off of Sadie.

Mrs. Skinner walked back inside, shaking her head in wonder.

"Sadie, what's wrong?" Bethany asked.

"It's him, Beth," she whispered.

"You mean…the one who…" she couldn't finish her sentence. *How could such a nice man do…that?* Bethany thought.

"Yes," Sadie whispered with fright. "Oh, I hope Zane hasn't found out. He'll kill him." Sadie's nerves needed to be calmed. She took several breaths to slow the rapid beating of her heart.

"I don't think he knows. I'll talk to Mr. Gates and let him know about Zane," Bethany said, her mind racing to think of what to say.

"No...I'll tell him." Sadie took a couple of deep breaths and stood to go inside.

"Are you sure, Sadie?" Bethany asked, standing in her way.

"Yes, I'm sure. Let's just finish up," she said determinedly.

"Okay," Bethany said, following her inside.

They entered the mercantile again and Sadie stayed near the door, scanning a shelf of books. Bethany scanned the room, then went to the front counter to ask about her order.

"Your order is in, Bethany," Mrs. Skinner said, pulling out two bolts of fabric. "Would you like to look at them? This particular shipment had a rough ride on the stage.

"Yes, I would. Thank you." Bethany pulled several yards out on each roll to see if there were any stains or rips. "They look fine. Can I have ten yards of each, please?" she asked, staring back at Sadie.

"I'll get it for you right quick." Mrs. Skinner walked to the back room to cut the yardage and found Seth staring out the window with tear stains on his cheeks.

"Son, are you okay?" she asked, patting his arm in concern.

"Yes, Nanna," he sniffed. "I'll tell you about it when we get home tonight." He wiped his eyes on his apron. "Do you want me to help you with that?" he asked, taking the fabric bolts from her.

"I need ten yards of each. I'll be right back to get them."

"That's okay," he said. "I'll bring them out." He got right to work.

Mrs. Skinner walked out into the store and found Bethany looking at the sewing supplies. "Seth is cutting the fabric for you, dear. Is there anything else you need?"

"Yes. I need a spool of white thread, a pair of scissors and a bolt of this lace," Bethany said, pointing to the eyelet pattern.

"Coming right up. What are you making?" Mrs. Skinner asked, pulling the rest of the supplies from the shelves.

"Oh, I'm making some new curtains for the entire house. It will be quite a project, but I like to sew." As Bethany made small talk with Mrs. Skinner, she kept a keen eye on Sadie.

"Well, I'll be right back with the rest of your order," Mrs. Skinner said, walking into the back room.

Bethany walked over to Sadie. She was still looking at the books.

"Did you find something you wanted?" Bethany asked cheerfully, yet with a clear tone of concern.

"Oh, I'm not really paying attention. I've been praying that God would give me the courage to talk to him. All the old feelings have come back, Beth. I know I said I forgave him, but I never got the chance to tell him in person." Sadie followed Bethany over to the sewing supplies.

"Maybe this is your chance," Bethany said, whispering a prayer of patience.

"This is not the place." Sadie cut her short, then thought for a moment. "Maybe I can invite him to church."

"That would be wonderful. I met him when he first arrived in town last Sunday and it seemed like he knew the Lord." Bethany was doing her best to encourage her friend in her time of need. She silently pleaded that the man she had come to grow fond of was indeed the changed man that he seemed to be.

Mrs. Skinner came out with Bethany's order and started adding it up. "Are you ready, Bethany?" she asked.

"Yes. I'll be right there," she said, turning again to Sadie. "Are you ready?"

"Yes. Let's get this over with." Sadie tried to smile her winning smile, but inside she trembled like a lost child.

As they were walking to the front counter, Seth came out from the back room.

"Hello, Mr. Gates," Bethany said cheerfully.

"Hell…, Miss Salister," he said, trying to smile.

Bethany could tell Seth was upset. "How is your new job coming along?"

"Fine, thank you." Seth didn't feel very talkative, but he tried to be polite in spite of the sickening feeling in the pit of his stomach. "Um…the ranch is really shaping up nicely."

"Yes, it is!" Mrs. Skinner said, smiling. "The Bar 'S' hasn't looked so good in years. This has been the first day Seth could come to town with me. There were more repairs needed than I thought," she said, shaking her head thoughtfully.

"I enjoy it," Seth said, relaxing just a mite.

"Good…good." Bethany felt the awkward tension in the air as there was a lull in the conversation.

"Hello, Seth," Sadie said quietly, raising her eyes slightly from the hole she'd been staring in the floor.

"Hello… Sadie," Seth replied, dropping his own gaze.

"How long have you been in town?" she asked, just barely able to remain calm.

"Almost a week," he said, nervously wrapping Bethany's order in heavy brown paper and tying it securely with twine.

"Would you like to join us at church tomorrow?" she asked, raising her eyes to meet his for the first time in twelve years.

"Oh, he'll be driving me," Mrs. Skinner said. "So, he don't have a choice."

"Yes. I'll be there," he said. *"Maybe we can talk?"*

"Maybe," Sadie said. "I…have something to tell you, anyway." She smiled and then looked away.

"Okay… I'll see you both on Sunday then," he said, feigning a smile. He walked into the back room and half-mindedly grabbed the broom. He was sweeping by the books when Bethany paid what she owed and they left. He stopped sweeping long enough to see Sadie's blonde waves flow down the street toward the saloon.

"How long have you known her, son?" Mrs. Skinner asked.

He thought for a moment. "About twenty years now. Before I came to the Lord, I hurt her real bad. I guess this is my chance to redeem myself." He went back to his sweeping.

"Maybe so. I'll pray for you," she said, patting his shoulder.

"Thank you," he said quietly.

✡ ✡ ✡ ✡

Bethany and Sadie walked toward the saloon. It looked and sounded like business had picked up quite a bit. Zane was on the porch smoking a cigar. He saw Sadie in the distance. She didn't look well. *Oh, well,* he thought, *she'll get over it. She usually does.*

"Sadie!" he called. "I'm sorry, but I can't leave just now. Henry's ailin' and won't be comin' to work." Henry was the second bartender. "Word is he ate something bad and has been spouting out both ends all day."

"That's okay, Zane. I've got some unfinished business anyway. I'll just ride home with Beth and come home tomorrow after church." Sadie did her best to hide her discomfort.

"Fine. I'll see you tomorrow then." Zane walked back inside the saloon without waiting for any further words from his sister.

Sadie followed Bethany to the livery.

"Hey, Bud!" Bethany called.

"Back here, Beth," he sounded off from the back of the stable.

"How much do I owe you?" she asked, opening her purse.

"Oh, it's on the house today. I love these beasts!" He hitched the horses to Bethany's wagon. "Oh, you had a pin come loose on one of your wheels. I fixed it up for you."

"Why, thank you, Bud. What would I do without you?" She smiled at him and led her team outside. She genuinely liked old Bud Rafferty. He reminded her of her father.

"Ready to go?" Bethany asked Sadie.

"Yes, please!" Sadie felt ill, but she knew God was working something out. *Lord, why is he here? Are we finally going to be able to settle this? Please help me.*

They hopped in. "Hey, Bud!" Bethany called out toward the stable.

"Yes, Beth?" he said, coming out to see what she wanted.

"If you know of anyone who wants to buy a wagon, let me know." Bethany picked up the reins.

"You sellin' the old bucket?" Bud asked curiously.

"Yes, I am," Bethany replied determinedly. "Oh, and I'll be needing to purchase a new one… something a little sturdier, that don't threaten to shake apart on that sorry excuse for a road leading out of town to my place."

Bud chuckled, "Sure thing, Beth," he said, waving as he retreated back into the darkened building.

Bethany flicked the reins. As they were riding out of town they noticed Sheriff Drake and two men riding into town. It looked like they were worn out. One of the sheriff's men was holding his arm like he may have been injured. *Wonder what that was all about*, she thought.

"Beth?" Sadie chimed, her stomach starting to calm down.

"Yes?"

"Thank you for being so understanding," she said smiling warmly.

"You're most definitely welcome, my friend!" Bethany flicked the reins once more to hurry the horses along. She silently prayed that the Lord would give her discernment. She didn't want to make hasty judgments where Seth was concerned. She hated to admit it to herself, but she was beginning to like Seth Gates. She never seemed to be able to forget his eyes.

✡ ✡ ✡ ✡

As Sheriff Drake rode into to town, he noticed that he and his men were drawing considerable attention. He steered his mount down the first alley he came to and rode up to the back entrance of the jailhouse. His deputies dismounted and tied their reigns to the hitching post. Drake remained dazed in his saddle.

"Sheriff?" One of the deputies was bleeding from a gunshot wound to his upper arm.

"Yes, Hanson?" the sheriff answered, still dazed.

"Can I be dismissed to go see the Doc?" Hanson asked. He didn't want to add to the sheriff's mounting anger any more than he needed to.

"Yeah…take the rest of the day off." Sheriff Drake waved his deputy away like he was an insect and dismounted.

Deputy Hanson walked off without another word.

"Denton!" Drake had dismounted and was taking the saddle off his horse as he remembered that his second deputy was waiting for further instruction.

"Yes, sir…"

"You may go, also. I'll see you bright and early tomorrow. We have some cleaning up to do." Drake headed for the back door. His heart was heavy and all tied up in knots with a jumbled mixture of both grief and rage.

"Sir?" Deputy Denton called.

"What!!?!... uh, what is it, Denton?"

"It… it wasn't your fault, you know." Deputy Denton feared for the sheriff's well being.

The sheriff hung his head, only looking halfway in the deputy's direction. "Go home, Denton. I'll see you tomorrow morning. Oh…" Drake turned to face the deputy more directly, "drop by and tell Hanson not to come in until the Doc says he's okay to work. Is that clear?"

"As crystal, sir." Deputy Denton nodded his ascent and led his horse down the street toward the doctor's office.

As Sheriff Drake set his saddle on the floor of his office everything of the last couple of days came crushing in on him. He plopped down in his chair, placed his face in his hands, and sighed deeply. "Sometimes this job's just too much…" He bit his lower lip hard, vainly struggling against a hot flood of tears.

CHAPTER 11

THE TRUTH HURTS

Mrs. Skinner decided to close the store early that day. She felt Seth needed to talk and she always believed friends and family came before work. They finished cleaning up and counted the money in silence. Mrs. Skinner could tell that Seth was trying to figure out how to tell her what he thought she needed to know. She was a patient woman and would wait.

Seth could tell Nanna wanted to know what was bothering him. He knew this day would come, but he didn't think it would sneak up on him. *Lord*, he silently prayed. *Give me the strength and the words to tell Nanna what I need to. And, Lord...please help me to mend the bridge I burned so many years ago with Sadie.* He finished cleaning up and went out back to hitch the horses.

As Seth was putting the reins on their safety hook he heard a horse coming up the street. He walked back into the store and saw Nanna through the front window talking to Sheriff Drake. He walked out front to hear what was up.

"Well, Sheriff. Did my information help?" Seth was being as calm as possible.

"Yes, it did, Mr. Gates. We found him up at Pesache Mine. He was camped out inside with a couple of buddies." The sheriff was worn out and ready to just crawl in bed. Seth could tell he had been in some kind of brawl.

"Is everything all right?" Seth asked, wondering what the sheriff was trying to say.

"Now it is. I was just tellin' Nanna to take that there poster off the wall. We won't be needin' it no more." Sheriff Drake turned to go. "Look, I gotta' get home. I've given my deputies the rest of the day off and I'm pretty beat myself. I'll see you around." The sheriff rode slowly down the street, his head hanging low.

"You mean...they caught him?" Seth asked Nanna in a surprised tone of voice.

"He told me the mine caved in on the criminals while they were havin' a shoot out," Mrs. Skinner said as she walked through the front door, locking it behind her.

"Really?" Seth was shocked. He didn't think his information would cause someone's death.

Mrs. Skinner noticed the pained look on Seth's face. "It wasn't your fault, Seth. Things just happen sometimes." She walked out through the back door and put her things in the wagon.

Seth followed, securing the back door behind him. He helped Mrs. Skinner into the wagon, hopped up next to her, and took hold of the reins.

They were halfway home when Seth decided that the time had come to tell Nanna about Sadie.

"Nanna?" he spoke softly.

"Yes, Seth?"

"Are you one to judge on first impressions?" He was hoping she would say no.

She thought for a moment. "No, I guess I'm not. I give a person a fair amount of time to get to know them before I make any judgments." She was really curious now.

"Well...what I'm about to tell you may frighten you, but I would ask that you hold your opinions and 'judgments' until the end, okay?" he asked.

"Fair enough," she said.

"When I met Sadie Alan, I was about twelve years old. I thought she was the prettiest thing I had ever laid eyes on. Well, needless to say, I fell in love. From that moment on, she was the one for me. I wanted to marry her someday and have a family and grow old with her and all that."

"You know, I wasn't exactly the most perfect kid though. I'm the youngest of four boys and my mama died giving birth to me. I wish I could have known her. Maybe that would have changed things."

He stared thoughtfully down the road for a moment. Sighing, he continued. "My father was the pastor of our church and my three older brothers were 'called' to be evangelists; you know, those preachers that travel from one hick town to another with tents and such. Well...*I* decided to be the rebellious one. I made all sorts of trouble all through school and embarrassed my father in services from time to time. I guess I hitched myself to that wagon when I was old enough to understand that my father blamed me for my mama's death. When I got serious about life, I could tell that bitterness was eating away my father's joy of living. But...instead of takin' the narrow road, I slid into that same ditch; anger, bitterness and hatred."

Seth looked over at Nanna, who just smiled sweetly. "The only thing that brightened my life was the thought -- and sight -- of Sadie. When I turned fourteen, I decided to try and make her pay attention to me. I behaved *proper* in church. I was an *angel* at school; even got straight A's. I even offered to help out at the livery on the weekends to save up money. But it was all in vain. Sadie always refused when I asked if I could come calling. She said that she never liked me more than just a friend. She was awfully polite but awfully firm."

"Well, the last 'no' I heard was on my twentieth birthday. I thought she might go out *as a friend* and help me celebrate. Not a chance! That was the final straw. I got so angry that something inside me snapped like a dry twig. I vowed I would get back at her for all those times she'd hurt me."

Seth's knuckles were white with tension as he pushed on. "The next day, I rode out to her place at a time I knew she would be alone. Sure enough, her brother was at work and her parents weren't around that I could tell. She was out in their back pasture brushing down Zane's horse. For a moment, I just stood and watched her. She was so beautiful! I just wanted to take that moment and capture it in my mind for all time. Finally...I sneaked up behind her...and...and...took advantage of her."

Seth was trying to catch his breath. His chest felt tight. "I stole her innocence," he choked out, "something she could never get back." He clenched his jaw tightly, attempting to compose himself.

"When I left there, I felt like there was nothing left to live for. The one thing I wanted more than anything was now broken and couldn't be mended...and I was the one who busted it. I felt so awful. There was a bad taste in my mouth; a rock in my gut. My hands felt dirty no matter how many times I washed them. I just felt like an empty shell."

Seth's composure was returning. "A year went by and nothing had been said or done. I had warned her that I would kill her and her family if she talked and I guess she believed me; until my father decided to preach one Sunday on forgiveness. I played sick that day because I didn't want to hear about forgiving. As far as I was concerned, what I had done was unforgivable."

"Sadie felt differently, though. She kept going to church and after that service on forgiveness, she started being nice to me...but then she felt she needed to set it straight, so she told my father. He didn't believe her. What he did to her after that just added to my guilt. He called her names. He banished her and her family from the church. He even got the townspeople talking so they would hate her family."

"The day she moved, I wanted to kill myself. I was so sick with guilt that I ran away. I flat out ran until I got to the next town. Then I ran some more. When my feet were all blistered and I couldn't breathe anymore, I stopped at the edge of the next town. I figured I had enough money on me that I could stay at the local boarding house for at least one night.

The owner was a fine Christian woman. She prayed for her tenants. When I was caught by her one night holding a knife to my throat, she prayed with me. She talked about Jesus and His saving grace and made Him sound more real than anything I'd heard in my lifetime of church going. I realized right then that I had to set things straight. I went back home and tried to find out where Sadie had moved to, but no one knew."

Seth paused for a moment to look at his surroundings and slow the horses. "I told my father it was all true and I watched the light die in his eyes. It never returned…That winter he died a lonely, bitter, angry man. My brothers were all happy about my coming to the Lord, but they never knew about this whole thing with Sadie. After we buried my father, my brothers all left on their crusades and I set out on the road to do whatever God asked of me. I've been drifting ever since."

When Seth finished talking, they were rolling through the front gate of the Bar 'S'. Seth's emotions were spent and he was drained of most of his physical strength. Mrs. Skinner had silently wept the whole ride home. When they stopped in front of the ranch home, she got out of the wagon and went inside without saying a word.

Seth didn't know if he would have a home or a job after that. He knew Nanna would be shocked. "Lord," he prayed. "Please let her turn to You for her answers. I know I've put an awful burden on her."

He unhitched the team and went into the bunkhouse. So desperately tired, he fell into a restless sleep; waking every hour to nightmares of the event that changed his life so many years ago.

When the moon had risen high in the sky, he got up and sat in front of the hearth with his Bible. He needed to pray about the coming day. He didn't sleep the rest of that night.

What Seth didn't understand yet was that God was cleaning the last remnants of blackness from his heart, and replacing it with Christ's compassion to stand for his faith no matter what the cost.

CHAPTER 12

HEALING SHORES FELLOWSHIP

Sunday morning dawned with fair skies. A chilly breeze blew up from the cove, dragging the morning mists in tow. The gulls and the crows added their voices to the seaside chorus as golden light spilled through the forest and meadows east of town.

Reverend Dale Cochran always arrived at the humble little white church on the town's highest hill bright and early. He wanted to make sure there was always a fresh bouquet of flowers on the table in the foyer. He picked them from his own garden every week while they were in bloom. He also wanted to have ample time to pray for the morning's service.

This morning, though, he sensed that God was changing things. He hadn't sensed this kind of change in the twenty-odd years that he had been pastoring the 'Healing Shores Fellowship'. It was like the wind suddenly changing direction. He had the oddest sense of some unnamed importance to this particular Sunday morning.

"Lord," he prayed, kneeling at the front altar. "whatever may come, your will be done."

He finished praying and rose, retiring to his office. His office door was right next to the front door. As he entered, he thought that he could hear someone coming up the front steps. Bemusedly, he swung open the door and saw Bethany and Sadie approaching.

"Well, ladies, this is indeed a surprise!" he said, smiling. "Service isn't for another hour and a half. What can I do for you?" He led them into his office.

"Reverend, we were wondering…" Sadie stammered.

"Yes?" he said, resting in his chair.

"We were wondering...if you would pray for us." Sadie sat in the chair opposite the Reverend's desk and stared at the Bible in her lap.

"Pray about what, Sadie?" Reverend Cochran was always smiling; at least when he was at the church. Hardly ever when he was fishing...

"Well...twelve years ago..." she quickly related the tragic event that changed her life.

"That... that is a moving story, Sadie," he half-stammered. Pulling out a handkerchief from the top drawer of his desk, he dabbed thoughtfully at the corners of his moist eyes. "How can I pray for you?"

"Well, you see, that young man, he's here... in town." Sadie relaxed. "He works...for Mrs. Skinner. Beth says that she met him when he came into town a week ago."

"Yes, and he seems... like he's now a strong man of God. I don't see that he's going to be a problem." Bethany was anxious to talk to Seth, too. She wanted to make sure that her feelings for him were not some girlish fantasy.

"Well, anyway, he told me yesterday that he wanted to talk to me today." Sadie became nervous again. "I forgave him a long time ago, but I never was able to tell him face to face. Now that I have the chance, I find all the old feelings returning and it frightens me." She was wringing her hands now.

"What sort of feelings?" Reverend Cochran asked, taking notes.

"Anger, bitterness, loneliness, guilt. When it first happened, my brother believed that it was my fault and after a while, so did I." Sadie was trying to keep her composure.

"Is *that* why Zane won't come to services?" The Reverend felt pity for Zane. He really wished he would come to service just once.

"Yes. Zane lost all trust in God." Sadie looked down at her hands.

"Why?" asked the Reverend.

"This man… well, he was the pastor's son." Sadie was thinking of her brother's empty life. "If Zane finds out he's in town, he'll kill him. I know he will."

Reverend Cochran shook his head, trying to decipher how life could sometimes become such a mess. "Well, let's go into prayer and we will see where the Lord leads us." They lowered their heads and prayed until the first of the parishioners were stepping through the doors.

✾ ✾ ✾ ✾

Seth dozed off about thirty minutes before dawn. When the sun shone through the eastern window he woke with a start, remembering today would direct his path from now on.

He cleaned up and walked outside to feed the chickens and horses. He took a look at his surroundings and said a prayer of thanks. "Lord, thank you for the strength to make this place what it once was. I am so thankful you led me here and I pray that you direct my path today as I speak to Sadie. Prepare her heart for your peace and understanding…"

Seth continued to pray a few more moments, fully unaware of the lone figure on the porch watching him and praying as well.

Lord, Mrs. Skinner silently prayed. *What shall I do? I don't want to boot him out because of something he did twelve years ago. How can I trust him?* She waited a moment. She felt a peace in her heart that she hadn't felt in a long time. *Okay, Lord. I'll trust him as long as you give me the strength.* She rang the bell for breakfast and waited on the porch for Seth.

"Good morning, Nanna," Seth greeted, quietly.

"Good morning, Seth. I'm sorry I ran out on you last night. I didn't even say good night." She looped her arm through his.

"That's okay. I realize it was overwhelming. I'm sorry." He spoke in a subdued tone, half to Nanna and half to the floorboards.

"Don't be, son. You're right...it *was* overwhelming, but I believe you have changed from what you were then. All you have shown me is kindness, hard work, loyalty and a strong love for the Lord and His Word. How can I stain that image of you by holding the past against you." They walked inside. "Let's eat and then we'll be off for church," she said, bringing a fine breakfast to the table.

"Thank you, Nanna," Seth said, staring at the linen tablecloth and its complement of biscuits, jelly, ham, and poached eggs.

"Don't thank me...thank the Lord," she said, sitting in her favorite chair.

"I already have," he said, taking her hand in his.

"Then, let's thank him for this fine meal," she concluded, bowing her head.

Seth prayed for the meal and started dishing up his plate. Nanna made the best sourdough biscuits ever to cross his lips. And a generous spreading of tart jelly made from the wild Oregon grapes which grew along the wooded trails near town really woke the taste buds.

"Nanna, can I ask you a question?" Seth was obviously avoiding her eyes.

"Sure, son," she said, smiling.

"How long have you known Sadie?"

"I've known her since she and her family came to this town 'bout ten years ago. It's just her and her brother now." She took a bite of ham, followed by a slow sip of coffee. "He's the one I told you about before; the hot-head that owns the saloon."

Seth's face turned ashen and he lost his appetite. "I didn't make the connection before. He went by a different name when I knew him." He pushed his plate back. "Ever since you told me about him, I've felt the Lord leading me to be a friend to him, but..." he trailed off.

"But what, Seth?" Mrs. Skinner was curious.

"He'll literally kill me if he finds out that I'm in town. Zane used to be more involved in the church than Sadie. But…after what I did…he never returned. I guess he's still angry." Seth took a deep breath and let it out slowly, barely nibbling the corner of his biscuit.

"Well, that'll just have to be up to the Lord what happens with him. The good Lord's in control anyway." Mrs. Skinner cleared the table and washed the dishes in short order.

Seth dried the dishes and they both reached for their Bibles.

"Oh, wait a minute," Mrs. Skinner said. "I forgot something." She ran back in the house and was gone for several minutes.

Seth hitched the team and waited for her in the wagon.

She came out with a big smile on her face. Seth helped her into the wagon.

"Seth, I have something for you," she said, pulling out a small leather pouch.

"You don't owe me anything, Nanna," he said, holding up his hands in protest.

"Yes, I do. You have worked so hard this week to put the Bar 'S' back together. Oh, and the store! You have really been a big help to me." She was getting excited. "I have decided that if all goes well today and you stay on here, that I will pay you ten dollars a week. So, here's your first week's pay." She handed him the pouch, smiling all the while.

"I can't take this, Nanna! You don't have ten dollars a week to pay me. Lawyers don't make that much, for goodness sake!" He was trying to hand the pouch back, but she wouldn't take it.

"Yes, I do have that much. Now, please take it, Seth," she said quietly. "I would be honored to share it with you."

All Seth could do was nod in reply. He deposited the pouch in his pocket, still not believing that she had the means to pay him this much, especially after seeing the state of the Bar-S when he had arrived. Resigned to his good fortune, he thanked her and flicked the reins to send the horses on their way.

✡ ✡ ✡ ✡

Seth and Mrs. Skinner arrived at Healing Shores with a fair spell of time to spare. Seth walked Mrs. Skinner up the front steps and then to her customary seat. She apparently liked to sit in the front…but not Seth.

"Nanna, if you don't mind, I'm going to sit in the back." She nodded her consent. As he started for the back row, he noticed Sadie sitting near the middle. They locked eyes for a moment and it seemed that all of time stood still around them. Sadie suddenly smiled and Seth looked at the floor, heading for the back row. He slumped in one of the back pews, hoping that the sermon would take his mind off of his awkward, confused embarrassment.

Reverend Cochran stood and headed for the pulpit. Everyone quieted down as Mrs. Petree finished the song she was playing on the piano. When she rose from the piano and took her seat in the front row, the Reverend began, "Welcome one and all on this glorious day!" Reverend Cochran always brought an air of joy to a crowd. Many perked up as he smiled at his attendees. "We will be looking at Psalm 25 today, although I am not sure if we will get all the way through to the end."

He waited until the rustling of pages ceased. "I will read the first ten verses and then we will go back and look at them one by one."

Reverend found his place and started reading, "*Unto thee, O Lord, do I lift up my soul. O my God, I trust in thee: let me not be ashamed, let not mine enemies triumph over me. Yea, let none that wait on thee be ashamed: let them be ashamed which transgress without cause. Show me thy ways, O Lord; teach me thy paths. Lead me in thy truth, and teach me: for thou art the God of my salvation; on thee do I wait all the day. Remember, O Lord, thy tender mercies and thy loving-kindness; for they have been ever of old. Remember not the sins of my youth, nor my transgressions: according to thy mercy remember thou me for thy goodness' sake, O Lord. Good and upright is the Lord: therefore will he teach sinners in the way. The meek will he teach his way. All the paths of the Lord and mercy and truth unto such as keep his covenant and his testimonies."*

Reverend Cochran paused to take a drink of water. "Let's have a word of prayer before we look more deeply into this passage," he spoke thoughtfully and deliberately.

Everyone bowed their heads, except Seth. He felt like the Lord had just stabbed him in the heart. He almost felt like he should leave, but stayed to wade through the conviction.

Reverend did as he said and went verse by verse. Everyone was listening, but not as intently as Bethany, Sadie… and especially, Seth.

When Reverend Cochran came to verse seven, the trio were especially attentive. *"Remember not the sins of my youth, nor my transgressions…."* Reverend paused and looked out over the congregation. He noticed the young man in back sitting on the edge of the pew; waiting for him to continue.

Reverend Cochran whispered a prayer for him and continued. "King David was always praying for the good Lord to not remember his sins; past or present. Goodness, I have all kinds of past sins that I pray for the Lord to forget." He saw several parishioners nod in agreement and heard one 'amen', but the young man in the back just sat stone-solid and pale. "One thing King David was sure of was that the Lord forgave him his sins. Oh, he was constantly crying out to God to forgive him, but he knew that the Lord did."

Reverend Cochran went on, but Seth didn't hear any more. He knew that all the old feelings of what he did so long ago would surface today. He was assured, however, that God had forgiven him and that was all he needed. Even if he hadn't quite forgiven himself yet.

Seth's conscious perception came in and out throughout the sermon. He heard the Reverend read verse eight which re-affirmed Seth's confidence in the Lord to forgive. *"Good and upright is the Lord: therefore will He teach sinners in the Way."* Seth felt layers of old guilt melting away.

Teach me, Lord, Seth silently prayed. *Teach me in your ways.*

Seth was now slumped to his knees in the back row, silently praying and weeping. He remained there until he heard the last verse, *"All the paths of the Lord are mercy and truth unto such as keep his covenant and his testimonies."*

Okay, Lord, he silently prayed. *I will do my best to keep your covenant and testimonies. Please, have mercy on me, oh God.* Seth stayed in that back pew after the message was concluded until someone tapped him on the shoulder.

"Are you all right, Seth?" It was Mrs. Skinner.

As Seth looked up he could see people were filing out and every once in a while someone gave him a curious look. He got up off of his knees and sat back on the pew.

"I'm...fine, Nanna," he whispered. "Do you want me to drive you home now?"

"No, I think I'll drive myself. I can tell that God needs to speak to your heart some more. Can you get home okay?" she asked, concern hiding behind her smile.

"Yes, I'll just walk if I can't find a ride." Seth was wiping his eyes on his shirtsleeves.

"Okay. Just tap twice on my door if you come home late," she said, rising to leave.

"I'll do that." Seth managed a small grin for her sake. His heart was broken and ready for the Holy Spirit's doing.

Mrs. Skinner left and the church emptied. Seth looked around and saw Sadie talking to the Reverend near his office.

Bethany came up just then. "May I sit with you?"

Seth motioned for her to take a seat on his left, blocking his view of Sadie.

"How are you, Mr. Gates?" Bethany asked, concerned.

"Please...call me Seth." He smiled.

"All right...Seth." She replied warmly.

"I don't know how I'm doing yet, Miss Salister." He said, leaning back and staring at the ceiling. He felt he should be honest with Bethany.

"Please...if I must call you Seth, then call me Bethany." She paused to take a good look at him. "Is the job going well?"

"Oh, it's the most wonderful job I've ever had!" he said emphatically. "I am most thankful to God that He lead me to this wonderful town. Actually," he said, snapping his fingers. "I should thank you, too!"

"Thank *me*...what for?" Bethany asked, surprised.

"You brought me to Pfeiffer's Landing and started me on the road to finding work. I couldn't be more grateful!" He was faintly smiling now and he could feel his heart warming with the breath of the Spirit.

Bethany struggled for words. "I... I was just trying... to be kind. I'm glad you're content." She rose to leave. "Well...I must be going. I'll see you around town." She shook his hand sharply and left. ***That was dumb!*** she thought.

Bethany tapped Sadie on the shoulder and motioned for her to join her outside.

"What's wrong, Beth?" she asked, concerned.

"Are you sure today is the right time to talk to him, Sadie?" she asked, looking back toward the door.

Sadie looked her friend over a minute. "You like him, don't you?" she asked, smiling.

Bethany blushed then grinned.

"Not that I blame you. He *is* handsome. Just…be careful." Sadie looked up toward the door. "I think I'll wait to talk everything out with him, but I need to tell him so. Will you wait for me a minute?" she asked.

"Of course, I will. I'll be right here in the wagon."

"Okay. I'll be right back." Sadie walked up the steps and entered the church once more. She saw Reverend Cochran talking intently with Seth. She didn't want to disturb them so she left.

"That was short," Bethany said as Sadie climbed into the wagon.

"Reverend Cochran is talking with him. I didn't want to intrude. God is moving here and I don't want to hinder what He may be doing.

"Good idea," Bethany thought for a moment. "Do you want to take a picnic to the Landing?"

"Yes. That sounds wonderful." Sadie smiled and the light returned to her hazel eyes.

CHAPTER 13

NEW BEGINNINGS

When Bethany and Sadie had first stepped outside, Reverend Cochran walked over and introduced himself to Seth.

"Hello, friend…" he began in a warm, cordial tone.

"Good day," Seth returned, too embarrassed to look him in the eye.

"My name is Reverend Dale Cochran." He extended his hand and Seth shook it. "I don't believe I have ever seen you before. Are you new in town?"

"Yes, sir. I just got in to town last Sunday." Seth sat up and tried to be civil.

"How do you like our glorious little shantytown?" Reverend Cochran was being as delicate as possible so as to let the Holy Spirit do His work. He didn't want Seth to know just yet just how much he knew about Seth's background.

"Oh, I love it here!" Seth was smiling now. "I work for Mrs. Skinner. She's so sweet. She reminds me of my grandmother."

"She **is** a peach, that Mrs. Skinner." Reverend Cochran paused. "What is your name, young man?"

"Seth Gates."

"Gates." The old preacher thought for a moment. "I met a 'Pastor Gates' a few years back in Florence. Any relation?"

"My father…" Seth returned to his melancholy state.

"You don't seem too happy when you mention him." Reverend was waiting for Seth to open up.

"That's because I wasn't exactly his pride and joy." Seth sounded a little too sarcastic. "I'm sorry. I didn't mean to sound disrespectful. I'm the youngest of four and I turned out to be the rebellious one. He never got over it and died bitter and lonely." He looked down at the floor then closed his eyes. "God is working on me today about that…and other things."

"Something I can help you with?" the reverend asked, leaning in towards Seth.

"Yes." Seth thought a moment. "Today you were talking about how you can be sure God has forgiven you for something you've done wrong."

"That's right," the reverend replied encouragingly.

"Well, that part isn't my problem. Not really. My problem lies in forgiving myself." Seth pulled his knees up under his chin and wrapped his arms around them.

"Yes, well, that is one of the hardest things to do." Reverend Cochran was thinking deeply of how to explain. "Sometimes…*we* are our toughest enemies. God says to give up your life so that you may live."

Seth interrupted, "I *have* given up my life! I've been sacrificing my time to help others whenever and wherever I can for years and years now."

"That is all well and good, but that's not the kind of giving He is talking about. He means to give up control of your life; your decisions, your will, your faith. Let Him have these things, not just the sweat of your brow. He wants your heart, not just your hands."

"Oh." Seth was confused. "So I've been going about it all wrong."

"Works of charity are never bad. The reason you do those works is where the right and wrong is. See…God gave us the ability to choose. We can choose to do something for God or others or we can choose to do it for our own benefit."

"So…what do I do now?" Seth asked.

"Well, have you prayed to receive Jesus into your heart?"

"Yes, I have."

"Well, the next stage is to pray to give up your will to God's control." Reverend offered his hand to Seth. "Can I pray for you, Seth?"

"Yes, please!" he said, kneeling at the pew.

They prayed for a few moments and then Reverend Cochran rose. "I believe God will show you where to go next, son…if you know how to watch for Him. Read the Bible, pray and always look for God's hand in each and every situation in your life."

"Thank you, Reverend Cochran. I appreciate your help." Seth rose to walk out with him. "Can I ask you another question?"

"Sure," the Reverend replied, latching the door.

"Which way are you headed?" Seth sent up a prayer of hope.

"South…why?" The reverend was curious now.

"Would you be able to give me a ride as far as you're going?"

"Sure. No problem there. Mrs. Skinner is my neighbor." Reverend beamed with joy, for he wanted to continue to talk with this young man.

"Wow! What are the chances of that?" Seth smiled as they climbed into the Reverend's buckboard.

"Many…if you know who planned it," the reverend said, flicking the reins spryly.

"Oh, you mean God," Seth said, the light returning to his ocean blue eyes. "I get it now." He chuckled.

They talked all the way back to the ranch. Seth's heart felt lighter than air. He hadn't felt this free of pain for longer then he could remember.

Bethany and Sadie went back to Bethany's place to change and make up their picnic lunch. They headed out to the 'Landing' about an hour later. When they arrived, they spread the blanket and ate before doing anything else.

"This is wonderful chicken, Beth," Sadie said. "I don't get much time to enjoy cooking at home. Zane wants the same thing every night; meatloaf and biscuits." She was getting full so she started cleaning up.

"Thank you. I miss having someone to cook for. It gets boring after a while cooking just for me."

They cleaned up and put all but the blanket back in the wagon. They walked through the town museum and hiked a ways up the grove trail; content to be silent in their own thoughts.

When they returned to the beach, they just stood there and gazed at the ocean.

"God is so wonderful!" Bethany sighed. She closed her eyes and took a deep breath.

"Yes, he is." Sadie started walking toward the lighthouse. "Beth, I'm so glad I didn't talk to Seth today."

"You are? Why?" she asked, confused.

"I think God wanted us to talk to each other on His terms and in His time, not our own. I just wanted to get it over with and forget it ever happened, but God has other plans, I think." Sadie folded her arms and smiled. "I can feel that things are different now."

"How do you mean?" Bethany asked.

"Today's sermon was so powerful. Remember when I said that all the old feelings were coming back?"

Bethany nodded.

"Well, they're gone now. I believe I have really forgiven Seth and myself down in my heart." Sadie was beaming.

"What do you mean, 'forgive yourself'? You didn't do anything wrong." Bethany was really curious now.

"Yes, I did." Sadie looked at the ocean intently. "I believed it when people said it was my fault."

They walked on in silence until they reached the lighthouse. They rested on some rocks and watched the sea lions bob on the swells. There were a few tide pools where Bethany found some rather ornate sea shells.

"We better start back soon," Bethany said. "It's going to be getting dark before long."

The sun was setting and it looked like it was just melting away into the sea. "You're right. Let's go," Sadie said, hopping off the rock that she had been sitting on. "I'm getting chilled, anyway." She hugged her arms and quoted one of her favorite old poems, **Beyond**: "Over the far horizon, beyond the setting sun, there lies a magic moment, when sea and sky are one…"

Bidding the amber sunset a good evening, they walked back to their blanket. It was well into twilight by the time they climbed into the wagon to return home.

What they didn't know was that Zane was at home already, seething in anger; wondering where Sadie was.

CHAPTER 14

FAMILY CONFRONTATION

"**Where'v ya' been**!" Zane screamed when Sadie came home that night.

"With Bethany…at the 'Landing'." She was nervous, but ignored him as best as she could.

"How come ya' didn't leave a note 'er sumptin?!" Zane was still yelling and threw his cigar into the fireplace for emphasis.

"'Cause I didn't think you would care," Sadie shouted, glaring at her only brother in his usual drunken stupor.

"Not care! I spent da' las twelve years *caring* fer you!" He slammed his half-empty whiskey bottle on the table. "You have no respect! You just as bad as my bar tramps," Zane hollered expletives.

He stumbled over to the rocker and slumped down into it. He hated having to look after his sister all the time.

Sadie hung her coat, put her clothes away, and dressed for bed before she even so much as looked in his direction; all the while, praying for patience and strength.

"You're right, Zane," Sadie said quietly. "I don't respect you. I have no respect for anyone who treats people the way you do. The only things I respect of yours are your personal space and your material possessions." Sadie stood there for a moment staring at him. He looked so old…so beaten down. "You are so consumed with anger and bitterness that it's eating away at you. You don't even look your age. You look sixty."

Zane looked up at Sadie for a long moment. Sadie could tell that his present rage was fading into sadness.

"You need to give up the ghost of your past, Zane." she said, pleadingly.

"You know I can't," he said quickly, returning his gaze to the fire. His scowl had returned.

"Why not?" Sadie asked. "*I've* forgiven him. Why can't you?"

Zane shot a hot glare at her. "Because he took away the one thing I adored…" He looked again to the fireplace.

"Zane…I became a new person when I forgave him. Why can't you see that?" She was sitting at the kitchen table waiting for a glimpse of hope from her brother's countenance.

"You're still the same to me, Sadie; stained, bruised and beaten." Zane felt tired. He knew that was a cheap shot, but it was all he could think of to keep Sadie quiet.

"Very well." Sadie felt released of a responsibility that had been weighing on her shoulders for years. "I am *not* going to live in a house with a person who would rather be dead than live a life of freedom in Jesus…I'm…moving out…tomorrow." She rose to go to bed.

Zane jumped out of his chair, stumbling awkwardly towards her. "You can't do that!"

"I most certainly can. I'm an adult, Zane. I wish no longer to be treated like one of your 'girls'." She added a hint of sarcasm when she mentioned Zane's entertainment.

"Fine!" Zane spat out before he stormed out the front door.

A few minutes later, Sadie heard Flash take off down the dusty road toward town.

"God, protect him…for I can't anymore." Sadie took a deep breath and sighed. "Lord," she prayed. "Bring someone into his life that he'll listen to." She headed off to bed. But sleep wouldn't come. Every time she closed her eyes she saw a flash and heard a gunshot. She didn't know what it meant, and since she couldn't sleep she spent the rest of the night in prayer.

CHAPTER 15

THE SILVER STREAK SALOON

It was close to midnight when Zane reached the edge of town. The only sounds he heard were all too familiar to him; piano music, laughing, glasses clinking. He had owned this saloon for so long that it felt like a second home to him.

Tonight, however, he took his time getting there. He replayed the conversation he'd had with his sister over and over in his mind. He felt mixed emotions. On the one hand, he was angry for the disrespect his sister bestowed on him. She could be so pig-headed sometimes. On the other hand, he was becoming more and more depressed because Sadie was right; he was letting himself waste away to a hollow shell filled with anger, hatred and bitterness. The saloon was nice to be in when he wanted to drown his troubles in drink and whoring, but tonight something was different. All of a sudden, as he rode up in front of the saloon, he saw how much of his troubles fueled this place.

Voices in the back of his mind reminded him of what his life was all about before Sadie's life was rearranged. He loved God; or at least he used to. He used to be happy. There was a joy that used to be in his heart that would carry on through any trial. It was all there until Sadie was violated. Now, all that kept him warm inside was anger and hate.

"Zane?" one of the saloon girls called. She walked over to where he was perched on his horse. "Zane, are you all right?"

"Huh?" He came back to his senses now. "Oh...yes...I'm fine." He hopped off his horse. "Get me a whiskey, Em, would ya?" He walked right past her and straight to his office.

Zane just sat in his chair and laid his face in his hands. What was he going to do without Sadie...?

"Here's your whiskey, Zane," Henry said, setting it on Zane's desk. "What are you doing here tonight?"

Zane took up his glass and took the whiskey down in one swallow. "Sadie and I had another fight. I'll be staying here tonight."

"Why don't she move out if you two don't get along?" Henry asked, leaning on the wall by the office door.

"She *is* moving out," Zane said sadly.

Henry's eyebrows rose in surprise. "Well…maybe you'll have yourself some peace."

"Mm…" Zane started looking through his desk drawers for nothing in particular.

Henry took that to be his cue to leave.

"Henry?" Zane called.

"Yeah?"

"I don't want to be disturbed tonight. Could you pass the word?"

"Sure. Which room you gonna' use?"

"Honeymoon suite. Tell Emily she'll have to bunk with the others." Zane waved him on.

"Will do." Henry saluted and went back to tend the bar.

✯ ✯ ✯ ✯

The Silver Streak Saloon was jumping with activity. The poker table by the door was the focus of attention; six men from all over the valley were playing until they lost interest. The five girls of the Silver Streak were hanging on the shoulders of their prospects, hoping for a winner in their grasp.

The one gentleman free of entertainment was a regular at the saloon poker table. Sheriff Ryan Drake would occasionally join in a game to make sure the pistols remained holstered for the night.

"Looks like I picked a good night to be here," Sheriff Drake said as Henry walked up to the table.

"Why's that, Sheriff?" Henry asked.

"Zane looked none too happy just now," Sheriff Drake said. "I bid two dollars."

"Fold…" the man to his left said, tossing his cards down sharply.

"You're right. He wasn't happy. He and his sis had it out, again." Henry was interested how the others were going to beat the sheriff's full house.

"I see your two…and raise you two more." Bud Rafferty said, throwing his money in the middle… never taking his eyes off the sheriff.

The next two men folded.

"I call," the stranger on the sheriff's right said.

"I want to see you two's hands first," Bud said, pointing to both of them with a toothless grin.

The stranger laid down a three of a kind; all deuces.

Bud chuckled. "You called on three deuces?…Bold." Then he pointed to the sheriff. "And you?"

All was quiet around the table. Finally, Sheriff Drake laid down his full house.

"Nice, Sheriff…but it don't beat this." Bud laid down a straight flush. He gathered the pile of money and stacked it neatly.

"Nice work, Rafferty." The sheriff checked his pocket watch. "Well, gentlemen…it is past closing time. I'm afraid I must slip back into my role as law enforcer of this town."

Moans of faint disappointment could be heard as the men gathered their things.

"Girls, can I see you all at the bar a moment?" Henry called.

They all walked over, wondering if they were in trouble. "What's up, Henry?" Emily asked.

"Zane's in a snit tonight and don't wanna' be disturbed. Em?" he said, pointing to the veteran of the entertainment. "He's gonna be staying in your room and he wants you to bunk with one of the others."

"But, Henry," she whined. "What about my job?" She pointed to the man she was with.

"You can use my room, but then you have to leave when you're done." Henry started wiping down the bar and washing the last few glasses.

"Okay," she pouted and then smiled. "Thanks, Henry."

"You can bunk with me, Em," Lizzy, one of the other girls said. "My prospect ain't staying." Lizzy waved good bye and blew a kiss to the man she had entertained that evening.

"Thanks, Liz. I owe ya one."

The girls bid good night to Henry and headed upstairs with their prospects. Zane came out of his office a few minutes later to lock the door and turn the sign in the window.

"You gonna be okay, boss?" Henry asked, concerned for his friend of ten years.

"Yeah."

"You want me to open at eleven or twelve?" Henry asked, hoping for the latter.

"I'll open it. You can go home after you get up and then relieve me at your regular time." Zane leaned up against the bar.

"Okay. Do you want me to make an order tomorrow with Ms. Skinner? We're in need of a few things." Henry finished drying the last glass and put it away.

Zane nodded in reply.

Henry eyed Zane with curiosity. "Somethin' else on your mind, Zane?"

"Do you ever get bored with this job?" Zane asked, quietly.

"Sometimes...why?" Henry was real curious now.

"Just wonderin'," Zane said, heading for the stairs. "Good night."

"G'night, Zane," Henry bellowed.

When Zane got to his room and closed the door, he felt strangely empty. He knew what he needed, but he had no idea where to start. He climbed in bed with a moan, "Ohhhh, I'm getting too old for this." He was asleep a few minutes later. He slept soundly, but had some strange dreams. Scenes of that horrible day when Sadie was damaged were running across the back of his eyelids. Things he had forgotten; like his first drink the night of Sadie's attack. He ended up getting very sick that night.

He woke at dawn remembering every thought and dream from the night before. He tried to go back to sleep, but sleep eluded him so he just laid there staring at the ceiling and tried to think of a way to forget the previous day.

✿✿✿✿

Reverend Cochran couldn't sleep that night. There was too much on his mind; Seth, Sadie, Zane. What a strange predicament. He knelt beside his bed and prayed well into the early morning hours.

"Lord, where do I start? These folks are all so special to me." He was silent for a moment. He suddenly felt an overwhelming urgency for Zane's wellbeing.

"Father, what will it take to bring Zane back to the fold? I want so much for his suffering to cease." He prayed on in an earnestness of spirit that he'd seldom felt before... the burden on his heart growing stronger and stronger.

CHAPTER 16

GROWING UP

Sadie didn't sleep very much that night, if at all. When dawn mercifully broke, she got out of bed and decided to head for the barn. An old claw-foot tub was kept there for bathing. Sometimes she'd take cold baths to revive herself if she'd had trouble sleeping. Revive her it did, too, for the well water seemed hardly half a degree above ice.

When she had dressed and fixed her hair, she pulled the drain plug on the bath. As the water drained away, she went to collect the eggs. There weren't very many, but there were enough to feed her brother, whenever he returned.

She cleaned up the house a bit and packed all that was precious to her into two carpet bags and her saddle bags. She wrote a note to Zane, placing it at his usual seat at the table. She then left the house and saddled Ima, her mare. She took one last long look at her surroundings, wondering if she would ever return. She allowed herself to replay all of her memories in her mind of her life here on this farm. There weren't very many pleasant ones. However, she remembered the last moments she had spent with both of her parents. Zane would have to grow a heart before she would allow herself to enjoy his company again.

Sadie took a deep breath and let it out slowly. "Well, Ima…shall we head out?" She climbed up into the saddle, gave the reins a pull to turn her horse in the right direction, and eased her into a slow trot.

✩✩✩✩

Bethany was collecting eggs for the day when she heard a horse whinny out front. She set her basket down and walked out front to see who it was. The morning sun was in her eyes as she rounded the corner of the house. She shaded her face with one hand and squinted to see who it was.

"Good morning, Beth," Sadie called, climbing down from her saddle.

"Well, hello, Sadie." Bethany noticed the luggage Sadie had with her. Concern spread over her face. "What's with all the bags?"

Sadie hesitated. She didn't want to worry her friend. "I'm...moving out. It's just finally time."

Bethany was completely surprised. She didn't know what to say.

"I know it seems odd," Sadie said, trying to ease whatever worries Bethany might have. "But...I could *not* live another minute with Zane." Sadie tied her horse to the rail on the front porch steps.

Bethany was stunned. She thought Sadie would be loyal to Zane to the end. Perhaps she had been mistaken. "I thought you felt you had to stick it out for Zane's sake," Bethany said, in a confused tone.

"Well...he's still my brother...and I'll love him always, but..." Sadie paused, thinking of the right words. "I guess God thinks it's time for me to grow up and take charge of my own responsibilities.. and allow Zane to fully face his."

"Where will you go?" Bethany asked quietly.

"I don't know." Sadie thought for a minute. "I need to find some work and a place to stay."

"Oh, well you know you can always stay with me," Bethany offered warmly.

"No, no. I don't want to impose on your friendship more then I already have." Sadie headed for the porch swing and sat down.

"You never impose." Bethany pleaded. "Come on...I've always wanted someone to talk to and cook for. It'll be fun! It always has been when you stayed over before."

Sadie looked long and hard at Bethany, trying to see just a hint of something that meant Bethany was just being friendly. But, she only saw love.

Sadie smiled. "Okay! I'll move in with you. But, at the first sign of strain on our friendship, I'm gone. And I insist on fully earning my keep."

Bethany gave Sadie a hug. "We'll have so much fun!"

"Will you help me find some work, Beth?" Sadie asked quietly. "I need to start saving up some money."

"Sure. Want to start looking today?" Bethany asked, pulling Sadie's bags down from her saddle hooks.

"Let me get settled first and figure out what I'm capable of doing in terms of gainful employment." Sadie followed Bethany into the house.

"Which room would you like?" Bethany asked, stopping at the top of the stairs.

"I like the garden room," Sadie said, speaking of the room next to Bethany's. "It reminds me of the Garden of Eden."

Bethany set Sadie's bags on the bed in the 'garden room'. It was so named for two reasons. One was that the window looked out over the rose garden and the pasture, which was filled with wild flowers of all varieties. The second was that the room was decorated to look like a garden. The furniture was painted white and had wisteria painted on a corner here and a post there. The walls were pale blue with scenes of wildflower meadows and mountains painted here and there. There was an old bird cage in the corner by the window that had a plant vining out of it. The rug by the bed was a deep green and the curtains on the window were a clean, stark white which reminded Sadie of clouds.

Sadie took a look around. "Thank you, Beth," she said, hugging her best friend. "I'll never forget this."

"You're quite welcome, my friend. This is your home now, so please feel free to make it so." Bethany's heart was racing with excitement. "We'll put together a chore schedule after lunch."

"Okay." Sadie started unpacking her bags. She wondered little of her brother's reaction to her moving out. She would pray for him, but she felt God had taken the reins of Zane's life back and Sadie needn't worry.

✿ ✿ ✿ ✿

Zane came home at lunch time and found the house abandoned. He was secretly hoping Sadie was just blowing off steam somewhere and would return. But, when he checked her room, he noticed all of her things were gone. A flicker of anger came and went. He didn't have to pretend anymore. He sat in the rocker by the hearth and closed his eyes.

"I'm too old to protect her, anyway," he said. "Hope you find your dream, sis."

He wasn't in any mood to make something to eat so he walked out back. He had an old hammock strung between two cedars. He climbed into it and fell fast asleep.

Zane didn't stir once until he heard a coyote howl some hours later. It was well after twilight when he walked back into the house, rubbing his eyes to get them to focus. He lit a lamp and noticed a piece of paper with his name on it sitting on the table. He sat down to read it.

"*Dearest David,*"

Zane closed his eyes at that moment to hold back emotions that he hadn't expressed in years. His given name was David Zane Alan, but he hadn't been called David since...

"*...I know it's been a while since you've been called by that name. But that's how I've always remembered you. Before the attack, you were so sensitive and kind. You loved God and His Word and I remember when you vowed to be one of His 'children' for the rest of your life. But, I guess some people are weaker than others. I will always love you, brother, but until you let the Lord heal your dead heart, I will not be living with you. Take care, David. I'll drop by the saloon and let you know when I have some work and a place to stay. I'll be praying for you.*
Love, Sis

Zane dropped the paper on the table, laid his head in his hands and wept. He hadn't shown any emotion, except for anger and since Sadie's 'accident'. No one was around to see or hear him and he was too tired to hold it back any longer. He sobbed with all the hurt, bitterness, anger, and loneliness he had. He stayed seated at the table for more than an hour until his emotions were spent. Then he slid from his chair to his knees.

"God," he whispered. "I haven't paid you much attention in years…" He paused. "I'm too old and too tired to carry this baggage any longer." Emotion welled up inside him once again. "Help me," he whispered before collapsing on the floor in sobs once more.

When Zane regained his composure, he felt like a train had run over him. It was pretty late so he undressed and went straight to bed; forgetting he had to relieve Henry. Zane slept through the night and well into morning with no interruptions. It was the best he'd slept in years.

Around nine in the morning, someone knocked on the front door and woke Zane. He sauntered to the door, feeling like he had the worst hangover in history. He looked through the peep hole and saw that it was Henry's brother, Harold. Zane slowly opened the door, feeling like he was going to pass out. "What are you doing here, Harry?" Zane asked, groggily.

"Um…" he mumbled. Harold had always been afraid of Zane. "Henry was wondering if you're comin' in."

"Tell Henry I'm sick and I'll be out for the whole week." Zane's head hurt, but his mind was clear. "I won't be back until Monday. Tell him he can do what he thinks necessary with the saloon."

"Okay…hope you get better soon." Harold hopped on his horse and left before Zane could give a reply.

"Boy…he left in a hurry." Zane shut the door and walked over to the wash basin.

"I need to get away for a while," he said to himself. He washed up, got dressed, ate and went out to the barn. He walked into the tack room and found an old bed roll and an extra saddle bag. In an hour, his horse was packed up with everything he could think of for a week in the wilderness. He hopped on his mount and headed for the foothills, not even thinking twice about his responsibilities. *I'll get out of everyone's way for a while. Besides*, he thought as he rode. *I haven't had time to myself since ma and pa died.*

✡ ✡ ✡ ✡

Sadie was sitting on the front porch drinking coffee when she saw Harold Lynes ride by. *He must be going to wake up Zane*, she thought to herself.

About twenty minutes later, she saw him ride back toward town. Zane wasn't with him.

Sadie sighed. *He's probably drunk*, she thought and walked back inside.

CHAPTER 17

THE CALLING

Seth felt like a new person! After that sermon on forgiveness he basically never left the Reverend's side. He wanted to learn so much about the Bible and the people in it. It was kind of sad that his father never thought to spend this kind of quality time with his sons.

Mrs. Skinner didn't mind Seth being gone so much. The chores were never neglected. She even had time to work on her hobby; tatting (a form of crocheting that takes limber fingers and a magnifying glass).

It was Wednesday night before Seth came in and actually stayed for supper. He walked into the dining room as Mrs. Skinner was just sitting down to eat.

"Hello, Nanna," he said cheerfully, kissing her on the forehead.

"Howdy, Seth! How was the study tonight?" She loved hearing Seth talk about the Lord. It was like having her own live-in preacher.

"Oh, I'm learning so much! I just can't seem to get enough!" Seth fixed himself a sandwich and sat at the table. "Have you blessed the meal yet?"

"No. You go ahead." Mrs. Skinner bowed her head and waited.

"Lord," Seth took a deep breath to calm his racing heart. "We thank you for this day and for this wonderful food. May you bless the hands that prepared it…and Lord?" he paused. "Show me what you want me to do for you. In your son Jesus Christ's name, amen."

"Amen," Mrs. Skinner whispered.

They ate in silence for a moment. Then Mrs. Skinner had an idea. "Seth, you were just praying for direction, right?" She was curious why the Lord would pick her for such an important message.

"Yes, I was. I want to do something for the Lord; something other than the physical labor I'm doing now." He smiled and patted her hand.

She smiled. "Have you given any thought to…becoming a minister?" She spoke very surely, but quietly.

Seth lost his smile.

"I'm sorry…did I say something wrong?" she said, taking his hand.

"No…I haven't thought about preaching," Seth said with a hint of sharpness to his tone. Then he softened with sadness. "I didn't want to become like my father."

Mrs. Skinner felt the prompting of the Lord and kept going as far as she dared. "But, your brothers are okay, aren't they?"

"Yes, except that their ministries are more like the theater." Seth was staring at his sandwich, losing his appetite every second.

"What makes you think that you won't be different?" Mrs. Skinner asked with confidence.

Seth thought a moment. "I don't know…maybe it's because I'm cut from the same cloth as they are. I just don't want to betray the Lord in teaching others about Him."

"What do you mean, 'betray the Lord'?" She had never felt the fire in her soul that she felt now.

"I don't want to be a hypocrite…like the Pharisees." Seth was picking at his food now, grateful for something for his hands to do.

"I doubt very much that you would be capable of that now, Seth." She was on a roll and Seth was listening. "The Lord cleansed you of your past when you asked Him for forgiveness and promised to follow Him. I've seen how you react to guilt. It eats you up until you feel you have to work yourself to death to make up for it. I saw and heard the repentance in you when you told me of your past. And look how much fun you have talking about the Lord. I could listen to you talk about Him all day." She took a breath and smiled. "Seth....I think the link has been broken. You can start anew."

"Do you really think so?" he asked hesitantly.

"Yes, I do." She looked him in the eyes with a confidence he'd never seen in her before.

"I'll pray about it." He didn't sound convinced, but he would follow through on his word.

They cleared the dishes and washed them in silence. They had much on their minds and didn't want to miss anything God might be teaching both of them through this.

They said their good nights and headed to their rooms. Seth took a walk around the property before turning in. He checked on the animals and secured all the gates; all the while thinking about what Nanna said.

"Lord, do you want me to be a preacher?" he asked boldly. "You know how I feel about telling lies. I don't want to follow in my family's footsteps. I want to be what you made me to be." He walked towards the bunkhouse now, suddenly drained of all his strength. Then he heard it. He froze in his tracks, ears perked. A single voice whispered, '**Rest**'. He knew it was the Lord.

"Yes, Lord." He went inside and got ready for bed. When he laid down, all he could think of was Reverend Cochran and his smile, standing behind the pulpit. He would talk to him Sunday about the idea of being a minister. He was asleep before he could finish his thought.

CHAPTER 18

BREAKING FALLOW GROUND

The next two weeks passed uneventfully for the most part. Bethany was sewing her new curtains and Sadie painted the living room and the kitchen a creamy off white. She also added sunflower borders to all the kitchen cabinets.

Bethany came into the kitchen as Sadie was just finishing the final touches on the last cabinet. "It looks so nice in here, Sadie!" She walked around the room, touching the dry spots like they were fine china. "What beautiful detailing."

"Thank you. Painting is one of my forgotten hobbies. I hope you don't mind the brightness of it all." After cleaning the brushes, Sadie took them and the paint containers outside and put them away in the shed where they were stored.

"I don't mind at all," Bethany said when Sadie returned. "It feels warm and inviting." Bethany put a pot of water on the cook stove. "What would you like for supper?"

"Surprise me," Sadie said, washing up in the wash basin. "But tomorrow, I get to cook."

"Okay." Bethany started pulling out vegetables from the ice box and spices stored in the cabinet next to the cook stove. She stoked the barely lit embers and added a few slivers of kindling, followed by a good armful of larger wood. A cheery little fire soon leapt to life. "Are you still going to town tomorrow?" she asked.

"Yes. Why? Do you want me to pick something up for you?" Sadie asked, pulling out her list and a stubby pencil.

"I was…just wondering if you would mind some company, actually." Bethany had her back to Sadie so as not to reveal her embarrassment.

"I don't mind at all! Are you going shopping?" Sadie was checking over her list, not paying much attention to Bethany's change in demeanor.

"No…I thought…" Bethany was hesitant about telling Sadie what she wanted to do. She didn't want to hurt her feelings.

"What is it, Beth?" Sadie asked, curious about her friend's task for the next day.

"I thought maybe…I would look for work, too." Bethany turned to face her friend. "What do you think, Sadie?"

"I think that's a great idea! We could ride in together." Sadie smiled that wonderful smile that made the whole world shine.

Bethany felt relieved. "That would be fun." She returned to the task at hand.

"I'm going to take a bath before supper. Do I have enough time?" Sadie started for the stairs, carrying a steaming bucket of water she had just removed from the stove.

"Yes, you have enough time. Supper should be ready when you're done." Bethany continued to chop the vegetables into bite size pieces. Dinner would be roasted chicken, carrots seasoned with herbs from her garden, and fried sweet bread.

✰ ✰ ✰ ✰

Zane felt alone. He was starting to hate his job. Since his trek into the foothills two weeks before, he felt like he didn't belong anywhere. He still maintained his rugged image in town so that no one would suspect anything, but he knew that he was changing. The walls he built around his heart so many years ago were coming down one by one and he didn't know what to do with this new sensitivity.

"Zane, are you all right?" Sheriff Drake asked, tapping him on the shoulder.

Zane was so startled that he dropped the glass he was washing. It shattered into pieces on the floor. Moaning, he grabbed a broom and began to sweep up the broken shards. "Yeah, I'm fine. Did you want something?" He resumed his task of washing the mugs and wiping down the bar.

Sheriff Drake could tell something was bothering Zane. He wasn't his usual charming self. "Yeah, Sarsaparilla, please." he chirped out in mock defiance. Glancing around, he noted, "It's not very busy tonight. Things okay here?"

Zane produced a scowl and simply nodded in reply. "You probably scared everyone off." He handed the sheriff his drink, spilling a little on the bar.

"Take it easy, Zane. What's up with you lately?" The sheriff was getting a little irritated. "Ever since your week off you've been actin' strange. Now what gives?"

"Nothing," Zane said, wiping down the bar again.

"Well, I'm just trying to keep the peace around here. Everyone knows that when you're in a mood, lead starts flyin'. Now…just keep it cool, ok?" The sheriff downed his drink in a few lengthy sips and motioned for another.

Zane poured another Sarsaparilla and kept to himself. He didn't know how to tell the sheriff what had happened on his road trip, or even if he should tell him.

The sheriff could see that Zane wasn't in the mood to make idle conversation so he joined a small poker game idling away at the table closest to the front door. Zane didn't care at the moment what the sheriff did so long as he stayed out of his way.

Henry had been working overtime lately. He didn't trust Zane anymore. After the trip he took, he had come back…different. "What's wrong, boss?" Henry asked.

"The usual." Zane didn't even want to tell his best friend what was going on.

"Family…family." Henry shook his head in disbelief. "Why are they such trouble?"

"I don't know. Listen, can you take care of things by yourself for a while? I need to leave early." Zane had to get out of there.

"Go ahead. We both don't need to be here." Henry took over the cleaning rag.

"Thanks." Zane left in a hurry, barely nodding at the few customers as he left. He was half way down the road by the time Henry looked out the window to wave good bye.

"What's up with him, Henry?" Sheriff Drake asked.

"I'm not sure," Henry replied quietly, still staring out the window curiously.

✪✪✪✪

The Cherokee Stage was just pulling into town while Zane was leaving. It carried its usual cargo; mail, parcels, supplies for the mercantile…but one thing was different. The Cherokee had a quite distinctive passenger getting off at Pfeiffer's Landing. No one quite like this had visited the town by stage in ten years. Everyone waiting for their supplies noticed her. She was rather tall for a woman. She was slender, but not too thin. She had mousy brown hair and a few noticed her bright blue eyes. She had a beautiful smile and she dressed like she was from the east coast; very prim, sophisticated, aloof.

After the woman received her luggage, she glanced around and walked over to the mercantile. Setting her bags down on the boardwalk, she began to closely examine the various postings on the advertising wall. There wasn't much there. She was just about to leave when Mrs. Skinner came outside with her broom.

"Hello," Mrs. Skinner greeted. "Can I help you with somethin', miss?"

"Yes. I noticed an abandoned building just up the road here." The woman pointed the way and Mrs. Skinner nodded. "Do you know who the owner is and how I might be able to make their acquaintance?"

"Yes, I do." Mrs. Skinner smiled. "I own it. Why do ask, young lady?"

"My, that is indeed fortunate." the woman said, reaching for her purse. "I would like to purchase it. What is your asking price?"

"Woe, darlin', not so fast!" Mrs. Skinner was intrigued. "What's your name?"

"Oh, pardon me." She held out her hand. "I am Melody McConner. Pleased to meet you, Miss…"

"I'm Mary Skinner, but everyone around here calls me Nanna." She shook Melody's hand.

"Pleased to meet you, Nanna," Melody replied, smiling.

"Nice to meet you, too, Miss McConner." Mrs. Skinner said, pausing to think a moment. "Now…why do you want to buy my building?"

"I would like to open my own business." Melody looked around at the people wandering by and noticed how overdressed she looked.

"What sort of business?" Mrs. Skinner was curious, but cautious.

"Tailoring. I am a seamstress." Melody looked quite proud of that fact.

"Well now. We haven't had a real tailor in this town for ten years." Mrs. Skinner thought a moment. "How 'bout I sell it to ya for one hundred dollars. Is that fair?"

"That is extremely fair. I was expecting more." Melody peeked in the store window. "May I buy out all of your fabric and sewing materials?"

"Of, course. I wouldn't want to be competition for ya'." Mrs. Skinner walked back inside and Melody followed.

"Will my luggage be safe out there on the boardwalk?" Melody asked, looking out the window every few seconds.

"Oh, yes. We don't have a problem with that kind of thing here." Mrs. Skinner walked in back to get some empty boxes.

"You have a nice store here, Nanna." Melody walked around looking mostly at the fine china and the books. "A good variety of supplies… some of them quite fine."

"Thank you, Miss McConner."

"Melody, please."

"Melody…my husband and I built this business from the ground up… quite literally."

"Where is he now?" Melody asked, curious.

"He…passed away." Mrs. Skinner's expression clouded for a brief moment.

"Oh, I am so sorry. I didn't mean to pry," Melody said, continuing to look around.

"Oh, that's quite all right. I'm fine now." Seth chose to walk out at that moment. "I'm not alone anymore. Seth Gates, meet Melody McConner."

"Nice to meet you, Miss McConner."

"Likewise, Mr. Gates."

"Seth is my assistant and my ranch hand." Mrs. Skinner's smile returned.

"How nice," Melody said smiling.

"Did you just arrive in town?" Seth asked

"Yes…would you two know where I could rent a room?" Melody opened her purse and handed Mrs. Skinner the money owed for the supplies and the building.

"Yes. There's a boarding house right down the street." Seth picked up a couple of boxes. "Where are these going?"

"Down to the old store, Seth. Why don't you load the wagon." Mrs. Skinner started wrapping the fabric and drawing up a bill of sale for the building. "Might not pass full muster back east in some big city, but we folks tend to do business with not much more than a handshake 'round here."

"Okay. I'll be right back to get the rest of these." Seth carried out the boxes first.

"Melody?" Mrs. Skinner chimed.

"Yes, ma'am?" she replied cheerfully.

"How did you find out about our fair little town?" she asked, wrapping the last of the fabric.

"I met some people in Florence that knew about Pfeiffer's Landing. They told me how the town was founded and that it was a lovely, quiet little place by the sea. I was born and raised in Boston and have always despised the city. I have been looking for just the right town to start my business and when I heard the story of Pfeiffer's Landing, I knew that this is where God wanted me. So…here I am." Melody was smiling as she told her story.

"You know the Lord, Melody?" Mrs. Skinner asked.

"Yes, I do. I have known Jesus as my savior for twelve years now. Do you have a church in town?" Melody asked.

"Yes, we do. It's just south of here and up on a little hill." Mrs. Skinner was glad to know Melody was a believer. "We have a wonderful Reverend and the church is always open. The owner of the boarding house Seth told you about is our church pianist."

"How wonderful!" Melody was excited now. "Perhaps I may ride with her to services, at least until I secure a Surrey for myself."

"I don't see why not." Mrs. Skinner was carrying the last of the sewing supplies out back to her wagon. Melody followed with her luggage. They dropped the supplies off at the new tailor shop and drove Melody over to Mrs. Petree's.

"Hello, Nanna," Mrs. Petree greeted cheerfully. "What can I do for you?"

"Hello, Ingrid. This young lady just arrived in town and needs a room."

"Hello, ma'am," Melody said, putting her luggage down. "I am Melody McConner." She extended her hand in greeting.

"Pleased to meet you, Miss McConner." She shook her hand. "How long will you be staying?"

"Oh, I am not sure." She thought for a moment, looking out the front window at her new establishment. "A few days, perhaps?"

"She just bought my old store," Mrs. Skinner chimed. "As soon as we clean the room above it and get a few furnishings set up, she'll have her own place."

"Oh, isn't that nice…" Mrs. Petree was looking at her register. "We are free of boarders at the moment, so would you like a room with a view of the street or the ocean?"

"A view of the ocean would be wonderful." Melody pulled out her money.

"Fine. That will be a dollar a night." Melody paid for three days worth and signed the ledger. "Right this way," Mrs. Petree said, picking up one of Melody's bags.

"Thank you, Nanna, for everything," Melody said, waving good bye.

"You're welcome, child, and welcome to Pfeiffer's Landing."

CHAPTER 19

CHANGE OF HEART

The next morning, Bethany woke just before dawn. She was too excited about going to town to sleep any longer. She was just finishing her chores when Sadie came skipping down the stairs.

"Good morning, Beth!" Sadie was also excited about the possibility of finding work. "Are you ready for an exciting day?"

"Yes, I am. But…" Bethany hesitated. "I think before we go, we should pray." She sat down at the kitchen table.

Sadie sat down next to her and took Bethany's hand in hers. "I agree."

They bowed their heads and prayed for the will of the Lord to be accomplished on their trek. Then Sadie got up from the table to make breakfast.

"What would you like for breakfast?" Sadie asked, setting the fry pan on the stove.

"Something light," she said, cradling a cup of coffee. "I'm a little nervous."

"Me, too, but if we just remember to let God guide us, we'll find work at the places He wants us to be." After a few moments of small talk, Sadie set two plates of scrambled eggs on the table and sat down.

"I know." Bethany changed the subject. "Have you heard from your brother?"

"No. I believe, though, that he's okay. I have this feeling that things have changed." Sadie smiled. "Henry's been worried about him."

"Worried? Why?" Bethany asked, curious.

"Henry says he's been too nice lately." Sadie giggled. "Zane hasn't been *nice* for years."

"Maybe our prayers have been answered." Bethany smiled.

"I'll believe that when I see it." Sadie cleared the dishes and washed them. Then they both heard a knock at the front door.

✡✡✡✡

Zane woke with a start. He had a bad dream, but, all of a sudden, he couldn't remember what it was about. All he could remember was the sound of a gunshot. He was drenched in sweat and he had a headache that would put the worst hangover to shame. He got up and decided that he would visit Sadie before going to work.

He washed his hair in the wash basin and shaved his beard; leaving only the mustache. He found his best shirt and his cleanest pair of trousers and shook them out. Then he polished his boots and shined up his silver belt buckle. He finished it off with his favorite hat; adorned with a silver hat band.

He had a cold piece of toast and a glass of milk for breakfast before heading out to saddle his steed.

"Lord, please give me courage," he prayed as he saddled Flash.

He picked some roses and climbed in the saddle.

"Here we go," he thought out loud. He took his time getting there. He was very nervous. Sadie didn't know about his 'change of heart' yet. At least he didn't think she knew. He tried to hide it from the town. They loved to talk about other people's lives.

When Zane rode up to Bethany's place, he was a little hesitant to get down off his horse. He did it anyway, though. He tied Flash to the rail of the front porch steps and straightened his clothes and hat. He walked up to the door slowly, so as not to alert anyone of his presence. He took a deep breath and knocked.

When Sadie heard the knock at the front door she got suddenly quiet and seemed suddenly nervous.

"Who is it?" Bethany called, noticing the change in Sadie's expression.

"Uh...it's... David," Zane said, chokingly.

Sadie gasped and ran for the front door. She threw it open and stood in amazement. She hadn't seen Zane so clean in years.

He handed her the roses. "These are for you...from the garden." He looked at the floor and asked, "May I come in?"

"Of course," Bethany said, opening the screen.

Zane walked in and let the screen slam behind him; all the while, never taking his eyes off of his sister.

"Um...would you like to sit down, Zane? Maybe have some coffee with us?" Bethany asked, trying to start a conversation.

Zane moved to the living room, sitting as close to the door as possible. "Coffee's fine, thanks."

Sadie sat across from him staring into his eyes. She definitely saw something different. She smiled as a lone tear streamed down her cheek.

"You're back," she whispered.

Zane nodded and smiled.

"What do you mean, Sadie?" Bethany set coffee and biscuits on the table in the middle of the room.

"She means...I've returned to the good Lord's fold." He took up his coffee and sat back in the chair he was in.

Sadie got up and knelt in front of Zane. "I missed you, David." Sadie hugged him so tight Zane thought he might choke.

"Now, I'm not sure if I'm all there yet, sis, so don't be calling me by my given name just yet." He hugged her back.

"What made you come back, Zane?" Bethany asked, holding back tears.

"Well…" Zane put his finger to the end of his mustache and twirled it; a habit he acquired when deep in thought. "After you left, Sadie, at first I figured you were just blowin' off steam somewhere. But…then I found your note." He looked down at the hat in his lap. "I finally decided to take a good long look inside and I didn't much like what I saw." A tear rolled down his cheek and he quickly brushed it away.

Sadie placed her hand on his and smiled.

"I prayed like I never prayed before and the Lord just…set me free." He made a gesture with his hands that almost looked like flying. "I felt so light. But I knew I still had things to deal with so I took a trip up into the hills for a week."

"What happened there?" Bethany asked.

"I camped near the old mine and thought I was alone." Zane got up and started pacing.

"Who was there?" Sadie asked, rising up and occupying the chair next to him.

"When I finished gatherin' kindling, a man came down the old mine trail and asked if he could share my fire." Zane looked nervous. "I'd never seen him before around these parts, although his face looked a little familiar. Anyway, when I told him he could stay for a while, he ended up pulling a pistol on me and robbing me of what little cash I had on me. Little snipe even took my biscuits…"

"Did you tell the sheriff?" Sadie asked, astonished that Zane would allow a confrontation to go that far. Usually he shot the person before they reached for their gun.

"Not yet. Anyway, after he took my money, he took off runnin' up over the hill and I never saw him again. I could tell he was just blowing through." Zane huffed and shook his head, slightly bemused.

"I'm glad you weren't hurt," Sadie said, relieved.

"Me, too." Zane thought for a moment. "The rest of the week was restful and relaxing. I prayed a lot and vowed I would start reading the Bible again. Except, I can't find my Bible, so I guess I'll have to get a new one." He smiled for the first time in weeks.

"How are you holding up otherwise?" Bethany asked, refilling the coffee cups.

"Well…" Zane paused. "I don't enjoy the saloon no more. I mean…Henry and the girls are still my friends, but…I can't stay in that place very long anymore."

"Henry told me he thought you were acting strangely," Sadie said, settling back into her chair and taking her coffee cup in her hand.

"I've been tryin' so hard to pretend to be my old self, but it ain't workin'." Zane fidgeted with his hat in his hands.

"Maybe that's the next step." Bethany was so excited, she ran to get her Bible from upstairs.

"What is she talkin' about?" Zane asked, almost to himself.

"I think she's trying to say that…"

"I mean that, maybe the Lord wants you to get rid of the saloon," Bethany interrupted.

"And do what?" Zane asked, genuinely interested, yet apprehensive.

"Do the Lord's work, whatever that may be." Sadie was excited. "Maybe you can go talk to Reverend Cochran today. We'll go with you."

"I don't know," he said, pacing once more.

"Come on, Zane. We'll go with you and wait for you, if you like." Bethany was silently praying it would be so.

"I want to, but…" Zane was nervous.

"But, what?" Sadie whispered.

"I'm scared, Sadie. It's been a long time since I've been in a house of God." He was heading for the door.

"We'll be right there praying," Bethany said, following him out to the porch.

Zane put his hat on and stared out at the countryside. "Okay," he said, heading for his horse.

Sadie and Bethany quickly picked up their things and hopped on their horses, which Sadie had saddled before breakfast. They headed for town at a leisurely canter.

Zane looked straight ahead; his expression looking more determined every minute. As they passed through town, he was silently praising the Lord that no one was at the saloon just yet.

Someone was watching, though. Melody heard the horses before she saw them pass by. When she did see the riders, she couldn't take her eyes off the handsome gentleman riding in the lead.

"Who is that?" she whispered. She was alone in her room so she was glad that no one witnessed her foolish schoolgirl behavior.

Zane and his two lady companions kept riding until they reached the church. It took a few minutes before Zane actually got down off his horse. He tied the reins to a post and just stood there looking at the church.

"This brings back memories," Zane said to himself, remembering the time when he saved the reverend from sure death.

"Do you two remember when I was here last?" he asked, never taking his gaze from the church.

"Yes," Sadie whispered.

"No," Bethany said. "What happened?"

"I was havin' a poker game at the saloon that night. It was one of the few that I participated in." Zane turned around and faced Bethany as he told his story. "A stranger rode into town and joined the game about three hours in. Well, needless to say, the man lost. He lost big time. All of us felt sorry for him, but he would have nothin' of our pity. He finished his drink and left."

"How did that lead here?" Bethany asked, pointing to the church.

"I had a feelin' somethin' was wrong so I had Henry take over closing and I followed him." Zane was relaxing. "He reined in here and for the longest time just sat here on his horse staring at the church. For some reason, the reverend was spending the night here."

"Actually, I had fallen asleep at my desk," Reverend Cochran said, descending the steps.

They all were a little startled. Zane went silent. The reverend told the rest of the story.

"I woke up because I heard a loud knocking on the door. I went to answer it and this man was standing there with his pistol pointed at my face. I backed up and let him in." Reverend Cochran was telling the story with excitement. "He asked…no…he demanded I give him all the church money and if I didn't, he would shoot me. Needless to say, I had no money with me. The stranger's back was to the door and at that moment, Zane came up behind him and clubbed him over the head with the offering plate from our foyer table. The man went down hard and fast. Zane took the man's pistol and I ran for some water and a cloth for the man's head."

"Always thinking of the other, aren't you, Reverend?" Zane asked, smiling. "The guy tries to kill you and you try to heal his wounds."

"Jesus told us to put others above ourselves, so I took that as an oath." The reverend was smiling broadly.

"What happened to the stranger?" Bethany asked.

"I tied him up and the reverend and I rode him back to town in his wagon. We left him with Sheriff Drake and the Marshall came and got him a week later." Zane sighed and then looked up at the church again.

"I..." Zane stammered. "I need to talk to you."

"Certainly. Won't you all come in?" Reverend Cochran led the way.

They went into his office and sat down. Zane thought for a long moment before he spoke. Reverend Cochran could tell he was serious about whatever he had to say. Sadie and Bethany sat in the corner, silently praying; so as not to disturb the work of the Holy Spirit.

"Well," Zane hesitated. "A few weeks back, I decided I needed a vacation."

"Vacation?" The Reverend didn't know what a vacation was.

"Yeah...time away from everybody and everything." Zane was starting to relax and remember the night he gave himself back to God.

"And why did you think you needed time away?" the Reverend asked.

"The night before I left...Sadie and I...had a fight." Zane was ashamed of himself.

"What about?" Reverend Cochran blocked out all other things in the room and paid attention only to Zane.

"I ain't never treated her with the respect she deserves and...well...she just had enough of it. She told me that if I didn't change my attitude...she would move out." Zane was trying real hard to keep his composure.

"Did you?" Reverend Cochran asked, barely breathing.

"No. I was drunk and set in my ways...until the next day."

"What happened?" the Reverend asked as he opened his Bible to the book of Psalms.

"Well...that night, I was so angry that I wouldn't listen to Sadie. I rode off on Flash and spent the night at the saloon. The next day when I got home...Sadie was gone." Zane was sniffling a little, trying to hold it in.

Reverend Cochran waited for Zane to continue. He didn't want to scare him into silence.

"I found a note on the table saying she would pray for me to return to the Lord's care and that she wouldn't come home until I did so." A lone tear streamed down Zane's cheek, but he quickly wiped it away with his shirt sleeve.

"That was the last straw. I dropped the letter, knelt to the floor and prayed what I could remember." Zane got up and paced a little and then sat back down.

"The next morning I told Henry's brother I was going away for a week and to tell Henry to mind the saloon." Zane took several breaths before continuing.

"I packed some grub and bedding and headed for the hills. I camped up there in the wilderness for a week with no one to talk to but the Lord, the animals and the trees." Zane smiled.

"That's the first time I've seen you smile in a long, long time, Zane," Reverend Cochran said, almost in a whisper.

Zane smiled again and went on with his story. "I set up camp and waited. After a little run in with this man who was hiding out up there, I felt like the Lord just made all the hurt go away. I had never felt peace like that before. When I came back to town, it took what human will I had left to hide my change. I didn't want anyone to know."

"Why not?" Sadie asked, startling everyone. They had forgotten that Sadie and Bethany were sitting there.

"Because…I'm afraid." Zane looked at his lap in shame.

"Is that why you're here now?" Reverend Cochran asked.

"Partly…I don't know what to do next."

"Well…" The reverend paused. "I think the first thing you should do is get yourself out of the saloon."

Zane smiled at Bethany, remembering she had said that very same thing.

"I think all of us should join hands and pray."

They all did as the reverend said and prayed for the next half an hour.

CHAPTER 20

FINDING WORK

When they were finished praying, they all knew what needed to be done for Zane's situation. The trio said their good-byes to Reverend Cochran and headed back to town. Sadie was smiling from ear to ear. Her brother was back. The two of them could start fresh.

"Sadie?" Bethany said.

"Yes?" Sadie answered, half listening.

"Do you still want to look for work today?" Bethany was still feeling a tug in the direction of finding work and she, herself, didn't want to wait.

"Yes, I do. The first place I'm going to is Mrs. Skinner's old store." Sadie rode up even with Zane, who was several yards ahead of them.

Bethany caught up and asked, "Why do you want to go there?"

"Didn't you see the notice on Mrs. Skinner's wall?" Bethany shook her head. "Well, someone rode in on the stage yesterday all the way from Boston and bought it sight unseen. They're going to open a tailor shop." Sadie was excited.

"I didn't know you were a seamstress." Bethany was secretly hoping *she* could try for it.

"I'm not. I want to offer my services in decorating the shop." Sadie's mind was spinning now. "What do you think, Beth?"

"I think that's a wonderful idea! Maybe you could open your own business in decorating." Bethany was happy. Now she was free to ask about the seamstress position for herself.

"I was thinking just that." Sadie looked at Zane and noticed a frown and a furrowed brow. "What's wrong, Zane?"

"I was just trying to think of a way to break the news to Henry." He wasn't looking forward to letting his best friend go.

"Maybe he'll understand," Sadie said, silently praying that God would give Zane direction and Henry would understand.

"Yeah…maybe." Zane returned to his own thoughts and headed off without the girls.

"What's the matter with *him*?" Bethany asked.

"He's troubled about telling Henry." Sadie was worried that he may not have enough faith yet to follow through.

"He'll be okay. I've noticed God's been changing him." Bethany tried to change the subject. "Um…have you talked to Seth yet? You know…it's been a while."

"I know. No…I haven't talked to him yet. I've been waiting for the right moment. He's been avoiding me at church. I just thought he was waiting for God's okay on the matter." Sadie thought for a moment. "Maybe I'm the one who needs to bring the matter up."

They were entering town now and just rounding the corner near the mercantile.

"Why don't you stop in and say hello? I'll meet you at the tailor shop." Bethany's mind was totally focused on her task at hand; finding work at the tailor's.

"Okay…but don't go in until I get there." Sadie waved as she dismounted.

"Fine." Bethany smiled and waved as she rode down to the livery to board her horse.

"Hey there, Beth!" Bud Rafferty greeted as she rode in.

"Howdy, Bud. What's new?" Bethany was preoccupied, but still remembered her manners long enough to make polite conversation.

"Not much. I won the game last night." Bud was smiling as he brushed down Bethany's horse.

"Again? How many times does that make?" Bethany was backing out as she spoke.

"Four." Bud was busy with the horse so he didn't notice Bethany trying to leave.

"Great...well, I'll be back in a while." Bethany waved and started walking out without waiting for Bud's reply.

"Hey, Beth. Wait a minute," Bud said, looking excited about something.

"Yes?" she said, turning impatiently towards Bud.

"I found someone to take that old buggy off your hands. You know...the one you told me you were selling." He pulled a small leather pouch out of his back pocket. "They offered twenty dollars and a trade of that buckboard back there," he said, pointing to the back of the stable.

"Wow," Bethany said in total amazement. "Who is it?"

"Me," he said, grinning a semi-toothless grin.

"You?" she said, once again in amazement.

"Yeah...with all this money I've been winnin', I figure I need to invest in somethin' of my retirement. I want to look more sophisticate." Bud handed her the pouch.

"I don't know what to say, Bud." Bethany was stunned.

"Jus' say you'll take the money," he pleaded.

"Okay, but that thing needs a lot of work," she said, gingerly taking the money pouch.

"I know, but I can handle it," he said, adjusting his suspenders.

"You got yourself a deal," she said, shaking his hand.

"Hot diggity!" Bud waved and started walking back into the stable.

"Bud?" Bethany called.

"Yeah?" he replied, turning toward her.

"I'll bring the buggy by tomorrow and we can exchange them then." Bethany smiled.

"Sounds good," he said, waving.

She waved and left to meet Sadie. When Bethany reached the tailor shop, Sadie was waiting outside.

"You been waiting long?" Bethany asked.

"No. I just got here." Sadie was staring across the street. "It's real quiet over there," she said, referring to the Silver Streak saloon.

Bethany looked over and nodded.

"I think I'll pop in when we're finished here. I want to make sure things are right between Zane and Henry." Sadie was real concerned.

"Just give it to God and everything will be fine." Bethany was looking inside the tailor shop window.

"Easier said than done," Sadie said, turning toward the tailor shop, too.

"How did it go with Seth?" Bethany asked, half interested.

"It was tense, but we managed to get a few words out. He's joining us for supper tomorrow night." Sadie peeked in the shop window, ignoring Bethany's surprised and irritated look she gave Sadie.

"Is that okay with you, Beth?" Sadie asked, smiling at her.

Bethany blushed. "Uh…sure. That'll be fine. You're cooking, though. I'll be a wreck."

Sadie giggled. "I think you're so cute when you blush."

"Hey, I sold the buggy," Bethany said, changing the subject.

"To who?" Sadie asked, half listening.

"Bud Rafferty." Bethany jingled the pouch.

"Praise the Lord," Sadie said, looking in the window once again.

Melody had a sense all day that changes were coming. She wasn't sure what kind of changes they were, though. After she saw the handsome rider that morning, she couldn't get the picture of his face out of her mind. She prayed for forgiveness for dwelling on unclean thoughts, but they wouldn't leave. She prayed all day as she was cleaning up the store.

She had just finished lunch and was washing windows when she noticed two women standing on the porch. She saw that they were staring across the street at the saloon. Then they both peeked in the windows.

"They must be curious busy bodies," she mumbled to herself, deciding to ignore them.

Sadie knocked on the door and then proceeded to straighten her skirt.

"She's in there. I can see her," Bethany said, smudging the window.

"Can she hear us?" Sadie asked, knocking once more.

"I think so," Bethany said, tapping on the window.

Melody couldn't stand it any longer. She threw down her broom and walked to the door, opening it with vigor. "May I help you?" she asked, irritated.

"I'm Bethany Salister, Miss..." She extended her hand.

"Melody McConner," she said, shaking Bethany's hand.

"We'd like to talk to you a moment, Miss McConner. Do you mind?" Sadie asked, wearing her best smile.

"About?" Melody said, not moving an inch from the door.

"We understand you'll be opening a tailor shop. Am I correct?" Bethany was returning attitude for attitude. Sadie bumped her arm.

"Yes. What about it, dear?" Melody was a little defensive now.

"Well, Miss McConner, I would like to offer my services in decorating your place of business." Sadie was confident that kindness would melt Miss McConner's defensive demeanor.

"I don't know." Melody softened a little. "I had my own ideas."

"I can help you with those ideas; make them come alive for you. It's what I do." Sadie was real excited.

"Do you have any samples of your work?" Melody asked.

That caught Sadie off guard and rendered her speechless for a moment.

"Yes, she does," Bethany said, as Sadie gave her a look that could kill. "If you would join us for supper at our home, you can see for yourself." Bethany felt awful for treating this stranger with such sarcasm. She softened a little and even smiled.

"Uh…good idea, Beth." Sadie regained her confidence. "Will you come?"

"I don't know," Melody said, staring at the ground.

"If you want to see her work, that's where it is. Is seven okay for you?" Bethany was starting to feel a little excitement herself.

"How will I get there? I don't have my own transportation as of yet." Melody was trying to be polite. She'd had a long day.

"Well, I have some other business to attend to in town. I can wait for you and you can rent a horse from the livery." Sadie was excited about the prospects of starting a business of her own.

"I'll run home and fix supper." Bethany smiled. "Is there anything you don't like, Miss McConner?"

"Please, call me Melody."

"Okay…Melody." Bethany looked at the ground and then back at her. "Is there anything…"

"No," she interrupted, smiling. "I like most everything. Can I bring something?"

"Why don't you bring dessert?" Sadie asked, smiling. "Mrs. Skinner sells ready-made pies and cakes."

"Fine. Where will I meet you?" Melody asked Sadie.

"I'll meet you at the livery at six o'clock."

"Wonderful! See you then," Melody said, walking back inside.

As Sadie walked Bethany to the livery, she thought how strange Melody had acted. Mrs. Skinner had told both of them that Melody was a believer.

"I wonder if that's the way all easterners are," Sadie thought aloud.

"Hmmm..." Bethany was deep in thought.

"Did she offend you, Beth?"

"A little," Bethany said with concern. "Now I don't know *what* to do."

"About what?" Sadie asked, genuinely concerned for her friend.

"I thought I heard the Lord's voice clearly on where I was to work for a living. Now I'm not so sure." Bethany was getting a headache. She hated all this confusion.

"Well, when we get to the livery, let's pray about it." Sadie was very matter of fact.

"How can you have so much joy? I don't understand the simplicity of it for you." Bethany was curious. She wasn't trying to insult Sadie.

Sadie smiled. "It's not as simple as you think."

They reached the livery and Bethany paid Bud for boarding her horse. Then they walked outside and prayed.

"Lord," Bethany started. "Please guide and direct us in what to say to Melody. We would love to be her friend, if she lets us. I pray she'll grow to love our little town and that she won't be too homesick."

"Father," Sadie continued. "Guide our hearts and minds in how to treat Melody. She seems real nice and I just pray that we seem that way to her. We don't want to be anything less than what you made us to be. Thank you for this opportunity and I pray your will be done in the matter for both of us. In your son Jesus Christ's name, amen."

"Amen," Bethany echoed. "I'll see you when you get back."

"What's for supper?" Sadie asked.

"I don't know yet, but we'll have a good one." Bethany waved, hopped on her horse and rode off.

Sadie sighed and headed for the saloon. *Lord, guide my words and steps*, she prayed silently.

✡✡✡✡

As Sadie reached the door of the saloon, she noticed Emily, one of the 'girls', sitting outside, crying. "What's wrong, Emily?" she asked, truly concerned.

Emily looked up and scowled. "What's it matter to you?!" she screamed. "It's all your fault, anyway."

"What happened?" Sadie offered her handkerchief, but Emily just pushed it away.

"Don't play innocent with me, Sadie. This was your doing; I know it. You've hated us since we came here." Emily was hysterical now.

"That's not true," Sadie said, a bit taken aback. "I never hated you. I just didn't like your profession." Sadie was trying to calm Emily down, but she, herself, was in shock.

"If you didn't hate me as a person, then how come you never talked to me or even just said hello when you came in here?" Emily was calming a little.

Sadie sighed. "I was afraid."

"Afraid! Of what? Some disease we might have or that we'd rub off on you?" Emily was angry now. "Sadie, we gave you every chance in the world to be our friend and you snubbed your nose at us every time."

Sadie was stunned into silence. Emily was right. *Lord, forgive me*, she prayed silently.

"I may be leaving the only man I ever truly loved, but I'm glad I don't have to see your pretty little face no more." With that, Emily ran inside, nearly running over the sheriff.

Sadie sat on the bench where Emily was sitting and cried. The sheriff stood by and waited for the right time.

"Are you okay, Sadie?" Sheriff Drake asked quietly as Sadie composed herself.

"Oh...yes, Sheriff," she sniffed and dried her eyes with her handkerchief. "I'll be fine," Sadie said, staring at the tailor shop across the way.

Sheriff Drake laid his hand on her shoulder. "It's not your fault, you know. God just saw fit to change things." Sheriff Drake smiled and set off for his office.

Sadie stood and took a deep breath. She feared there would be a lot of tension inside. She slowly walked in and looked around. All the girls were upstairs in one of the rooms, weeping. Zane and Mrs. Skinner were sitting at the table closest to the bar, talking. She walked over to the table and sat down to join the conversation.

"Ahh...just the person I wanted to see," Zane said, patting Sadie's hand. "Sorry about Em's outburst out there."

"I'm okay." Sadie smiled. "How are you, Nanna?"

"Just fine, dear. I'm sorry I couldn't talk earlier. I had to meet with your brother here." She smiled at Zane.

"That's okay. I didn't even notice you had stepped out. I came in to talk to Seth," Sadie said and then quickly put her hand over her mouth.

"Who's Seth?" Zane asked curiously.

"Oh, he's my new stock-boy," Nanna said, trying to cover Sadie's tracks for her.

"What did you need to talk to the stock-boy for?" Zane asked.

"About an order," she said, looking down at the table and then up at Zane. "What did you need to see me about?" Sadie said, changing the subject.

"Well, I'm not going to sell the saloon," he said, smiling.

"What about doing God's will?" she asked, concerned.

"I believe this is God's will. Now hear me out." Zane was excited.

"Okay, okay…" she giggled.

"I'm going to turn the Silver Streak into a full-blown hotel and diner. I want you to decorate it." Zane smiled and waited for Sadie's reply.

"What about Mrs. Petree's place? Won't you be in competition?" Sadie always thought of the one thing Zane forgot.

"Hmmm…I forgot about her." Zane thought for a moment. "I need to talk to her before I go any further on this. Excuse me," Zane said, leaving the saloon.

"What's going to happen to the girls?" Sadie asked, hoping Mrs. Skinner knew the answer.

"Your brother gave them all a chance to work here at the new hotel. All but two accepted; Emily and Lizzy." Mrs. Skinner looked at Henry. "Henry is going to be the restaurant foreman."

"What kind of work will the girls be doing here?" Sadie asked hesitantly.

Mrs. Skinner laughed. "Housekeeping, waitressing and cooking."

Sadie sighed with relief and looked around. She could already get a picture of what it would look like. "Nanna, could you tell Zane thank you and that I would love to decorate? I need to get home." Sadie stood and pushed her chair in.

"Certainly," Mrs. Skinner said, smiling.

"Good bye," Sadie said, turning to leave. "Oh…and thank you for helping me when I slipped about Seth."

"Not a problem, child. Good night," Mrs. Skinner said, waving.

"Have a nice evening," Sadie said, walking out of the saloon.

"You do the same," Mrs. Skinner called after her.

✮ ✮ ✮ ✮

Sadie met Melody outside of Mrs. Petree's as she was heading for the livery. The time had come for them to meet up and travel together to Bethany's house for their dinner engagement. "Can I carry something for you, Melody?" she asked.

"No, thank you. I think I have it," Melody replied, balancing two pies which she had purchased from the mercantile on one arm. Her cloak was draped neatly across the other. They headed for the livery and Melody rented a horse for the night. Realizing that she hadn't planned ahead in regards to the pies, she found herself in a bit of a quandary.

"It'd truly be a shame to see those pies of Mrs. Skinners' end up splattered on the road for the raccoons to find!" Bud exclaimed. He generously supplied the ladies with the use of a small utility wagon for the evening.

"We only live a few miles outside of town," Sadie said as they headed north. "We should be there before the sun goes to bed."

"It must be nice to live in the country. I have always wanted to." Melody looked around at the scenery as they went along, the little utility wagon bumping along behind.

"Were you born in a big city?" Sadie was curious.

"You don't waste any time, do you?" Melody smiled.

"I'm sorry. Was that improper of me? I didn't mean to pry." Sadie said apologetically.

"That's all right. I realize now that my first impression of you was wrong." Melody thought for a moment. "Yes. I was born and raised in Boston, Massachusetts."

"What was your first impression of me?" Sadie asked, hoping she didn't bore Melody with all these questions.

Melody giggled. "I thought you two were….the town gossips."

Sadie laughed. "Oh my! Bethany will love to hear that."

They reached the house a while later and tied the horses to the rail of the front porch steps.

"Whatever Bethany is cooking sure smells wonderful." Melody was a little hesitant to go inside because she feared that she may have stepped on Bethany's toes earlier.

"Come on inside." Sadie held the door for her and helped her carry the pies.

CHAPTER 21

BLOSSOMS OF FRIENDSHIP

Bethany decided that she would make her favorite meal for their guest; pot roast. She put the roast in the oven as soon as she arrived home so it would have time to cook to perfection. Then she prepared mashed potatoes and gravy, vegetables of all sorts, and a large salad made with greens and tomatoes from the garden. The last thing she made was her famous whipped eggs. Everyone she knew reminded her to bring her whipped eggs to every town and church picnic. She only hoped and prayed that Miss Melody McConner from far away Boston would also enjoy them.

As she was putting the finishing touches on the setting of the supper table, she heard horses ride up. "That must be them," she said as she lit the candle in the center of the table.

Sadie and Melody came in chattering like magpies in May. They hung their coats and saddle bags by the door.

"Mmmm...what smells so good?" Sadie asked, walking into the kitchen to wash up.

"Pot roast and all the trimmings," Bethany replied, stirring the gravy.

"Can I help?" Sadie asked.

"Yes...take over here," Bethany said, handing Sadie the gravy spoon,"...while I show our guest where to freshen up."

"I'll put everything on the table." Sadie set to work to do what little she could to help.

"Follow me," Bethany said to Melody.

Melody set the pies on the counter and followed Bethany upstairs to the washroom.

"All the painting and trim work you see throughout the house is done by Sadie's hand." Bethany was proud of her friend's work.

"Oh?" was all Melody could say. She, too, was fascinated by all the art work. "It does seem quite fine. And detailed…"

"Here you are," Bethany said as they reached the washroom at the end of the hall.

"Thank you." Melody was a little nervous. "Uh…I will be down in a moment."

"Okay. We'll wait for you at the table." Bethany left to go back downstairs.

Melody closed the washroom door. An oil lamp was already lit on a shelf above the window. She surveyed her appearance in the wall mirror.

"Hmmm…" she murmured, eyeing her hair. "I think I will wear my hair down like them." She proceeded to unpin her bun and let her mousy brown tendrils fall where they may. She pulled back two side strands and pinned them in the back.

"There…now I won't look so out of place."

She washed her hands in the washbasin and sprayed a smidgen of perfume on her wrists. Then she opened the door and slowly walked down the hall, examining the stenciling on the walls.

"She's very good," she whispered. She walked downstairs to join her hostesses at the supper table.

✿✿✿✿

Earlier that evening before Sadie and Melody had made their way to the livery, Zane was just departing Mrs. Petree's office. He glanced up the street and noticed his sister standing outside the boarding house. As he paced up the boardwalk in her direction, he suddenly froze. Someone was standing with Sadie, talking to her. She was the most beautiful woman Zane had ever seen.

Mrs. Petree noticed Zane's mouth agape as he stood there awkwardly. "Are you all right, Zane?" she called from the front desk.

Zane didn't answer. He was captivated by this woman's smile. She seemed to move with such grace.

"Zane?" Mrs. Petree followed him outside and spoke a little louder, trying to get his attention. Then she followed his gaze and smiled.

"Who is *she*?" Zane breathed.

"She is one of my boarders…A Miss Melody McConner." Mrs. Petree waited for Zane to look her way.

"How long is she staying here?" Zane's mouth suddenly felt dry as dirt.

"Hopefully, permanently." Mrs. Petree shook her head in humored disbelief and walked back inside.

Zane turned to face her. "What do you mean by that?" Zane asked.

"She purchased Nanna's old store to start her own business." She called back over her shoulder. "Uh…tailoring, I think she said."

"Wow," was all that Zane could say. He felt like he was in a fog.

When he turned again, Sadie and Melody were gone. Zane paced off, scanning the street as he went. He noticed the ladies again as they departed the livery; heading in the direction of Bethany's house.

"She must be eatin' at their house," Zane mumbled to himself. He snapped out of his stupor long enough to remember the business at hand. "Oh, I left Nanna hangin' at the saloon." He made his way back to the saloon.

"They both left, fool," Henry chuckled.

"Oh, no. Was Nanna upset?" Zane asked, leaning against the bar.

"No…at least she didn't seem upset. She said to tell you Sadie had to leave because she had company and that she would see you Sunday." Henry noticed a glassy look in Zane's eyes. "What's the matter?"

"I just saw the most beautiful woman I've ever seen!" Zane said, sighing.

"Really?" Henry said, setting his towel down.

Zane went on to describe Melody in full detail. "I even know her name," he told Henry proudly.

"What is it?" Henry asked, happy to see Zane 'alive' again.

"Melody McConner. She bought Nanna's old store to start a tailor shop." Zane was looking out the window now.

"You gonna' go after her?" Henry asked with a wink.

"I don't know," Zane moaned.

"Why not?" Henry asked. "Make your play… if you get shot down, you get shot down…"

"I want to start my new life on the right foot. Miss McConner isn't like our girls. She's sophisticated…and innocent." Zane didn't notice Emily was standing at the top of the stairs listening.

"*Thank you very much!*" she screamed in disappointment.

"Uh, oh," Henry whispered, leaning in toward Zane and grinning. "Undertaker's doing business tonight!"

Zane stammered in embarrassment. "I'm sorry, Em," he said. "I… I didn't…"

"I don't care what you thought you meant to say. I don't know what I ever saw in you. I hope you rot in hell!" Emily grabbed her carpet bag and stormed out of the saloon. She ran to the mercantile just as the Cherokee stage was about to leave. She handed her carpet bag to the driver and got on board. The reins were snapped and the stage disappeared into the twilight, leaving only a cloud of dust in its wake.

"I hope she knows I didn't mean any offense," Zane sighed with a heavy heart.

"She's just lashing out like a wounded animal. When she gets her life back on track, she'll forget all about it." Henry smiled and then retreated to the back room to take inventory.

"I hope so," Zane whispered. Then his thoughts returned to the beautiful angel he saw earlier…and he got a bright idea. He picked up his hat and coat and ran to the back room. "I'll see you tomorrow for the planning meeting." Zane was excited.

"What time?" Henry asked, not looking at Zane as he spoke.

"Ten in the mornin'…sharp." Zane left the back room and then came back a few seconds later. "And tell customers as they drop in that tonight's the last night of the saloon. After that, we'll be closed until further notice."

"Will do," Henry said, smiling.

"Thanks…see ya'!" Zane ran outside and hopped on Flash.

"Come on, Flash. Let's see if we can make supper in time." They rode off at full speed. Zane secretly prayed that he wouldn't act like a fool.

✡ ✡ ✡ ✡

Back at Bethany's house, Melody came downstairs just as Sadie finished filling the water glasses.

"Your hair looks nice that way," Bethany commented as she sat down at the table.

"Thank you," Melody said shyly.

"You can sit down there, Melody," Sadie said, pointing to the head of the table.

Melody sat down and placed her napkin in her lap. "This looks delicious," she said, attempting to break the ice.

"Thank you," Bethany said, smiling. "Sadie, would you open the meal in prayer?"

"Certainly." She held out her hands to both of her friends.

Melody stared at first and then slowly took both Sadie's hand and Bethany's hand and bowed her head.

When Sadie had finished praying, she started passing the food around. Then they heard a knock on the door.

"I wonder who that could be," Bethany said, rising to answer the door.

When she opened the door she couldn't believe the sight before her. Zane was standing there with dirt all over him and weeds in his hair. She started giggling.

"Hello, Zane." Bethany could hardly keep a straight face. "Would you like to come in? We're just sitting down to supper."

"May I join you?" he ventured boldly.

"Uh...sure. Come on in." Bethany waved him in and closed the door behind him. "I'll get you a place setting."

"Howdy, Zane," Sadie said, pouring coffee.

Melody thanked God that her back was to this stranger for she could feel his eyes boring into her.

"Hey there, sis. Um...could I possibly use your washroom to clean up a bit?" Zane suddenly felt like a fool.

"Sure. What happened?" Sadie asked, smiling.

"Uh...I took a short cut through the field. The horse dropped a hoof into a digger-rat hole and threw me." Zane felt really dirty and wished he hadn't rushed so blindly through the field to get there.

"Oh...well you know where the washroom is." Sadie shook her head in disbelief as she watched her brother retreat sheepishly up the stairs.

"So, Melody...when did you first learn tailoring?" Bethany asked, trying to start a conversation.

"My mother began teaching me when I was five. To her it was just a part of life, but when she taught me, I knew it was more than that." Melody started to relax.

"Do you miss your family?" Sadie asked shyly.

"Yes, but...I have really felt that this is where God wants me to be." She stopped in mid-thought because she heard the man they called Zane descending the stairs.

Sadie and Bethany looked at each other and smiled. As Zane sat down next to Bethany, Sadie spoke up.

"Melody, meet my brother, Zane Alan."

"How do you do?" Melody greeted, extending her hand and trying to hold in the butterflies.

"Fine, thanks." Zane shook her hand.

"Zane, this is Melody McConner. She's starting a tailoring business in town."

"Please to meet ya'," Zane said quietly.

"Likewise," Melody said, never taking her eyes from his.

"Zane, would you like some pot roast?" Sadie asked, holding the plate out to him.

He just sat there mesmerized by Melody's gaze. He didn't hear Sadie's question.

"Zane?" Sadie said sharply.

"Oh...sorry, Sadie," he said, taking the dish.

"So...what do you think of Sadie's work, Melody?" Bethany asked.

"I think it is wonderful! It is very bright and inviting. That is what I want for my shop, too. I want it to be...inviting." Melody took small bites so as not to seem an over anxious eater.

"What do you think of my offer? Did you have time to think about it?" Sadie asked, sitting on the edge of her seat.

"Yes, I did have time to think about it and ...I would love to have you decorate my shop." Melody smiled.

Sadie squealed with delight and ran over and gave Melody a hug. "When would you like me to start?"

"Why don't you meet me at the store about ten in the morning and we can discuss what I would like you to do." Melody felt strangely at home with these new friends of hers.

"Okay. Ten it is." Sadie started clearing the supper dishes. "Zane?"

"Yeah?" Zane answered, staring at his plate which had hardly been touched.

"Are you finished eating?" Sadie asked.

"Oh…" Zane took a few quick bites. "Yes, I am. Thanks." He handed Sadie his plate.

"So, Mr. Alan. What do you do for a living?" Melody asked, trying to calm her nerves.

"Uh…I own…the saloon across the street from your store." He stared at the table, too embarrassed to make eye contact.

"Oh," was all Melody could say. "So….you do not attend church?"

"I didn't before last week," Zane said, blushing. "Not for a long time, anyway. But I'll be startin' to this weekend."

Melody felt insulted. "Oh, so the only reason you would attend church services is to fawn over women?"

"Oh, no. Not at all." Zane paused. "I prayed this mornin' to receive Jesus into my heart. I'm closing the saloon tomorrow and remodeling it into a hotel and restaurant. I…I hope I didn't offend you."

"Well…I was offended at first…but it is not your fault. All my life I have met men who pursue me to church and only attend if I allow them to court me. I just automatically assumed you…were one of those men. I am sorry," Melody said, blushing. She felt as small as an ant. The west was very different from Boston.

"That's okay," Zane felt relieved. "If you had asked me a month ago, I would have been one of those men. But…I hope to change into something better with the Lord's help."

"Well…" Bethany spoke up. "Would you all like some dessert?"

Everyone chimed a resounding yes and Melody decided to help Bethany serve.

"Oh, you don't have to help me. You're our guest," Bethany said.

"I want to help. Besides…it was getting a little tense in there," Melody whispered. They went into the kitchen to cut the apple pie Melody had brought.

"What are you thinking?" Sadie asked Zane sternly.

"Whatta ya mean?" Zane tried to play innocent.

"I saw the way you looked at her." Sadie was nervous at what might be brewing in Zane's mind. She didn't want anything to jeopardize the friendship that was blossoming between Melody, Sadie and Bethany.

"Sadie, I'm not like that anymore. I just thought she was a beautiful lady and wanted to get to know her. That's all."

Sadie eyed her brother for the longest moment before speaking. "Just don't forget God's will in all this."

"I won't; believe me," Zane said, rubbing his temple.

Bethany and Melody brought in dessert and coffee.

"Melody?" Sadie started.

"Yes," Melody answered, handing a plate of pie to Zane.

"Are you looking to hire any other seamstresses?" Sadie winked at Bethany.

"Sadie!" Bethany whined.

"I am not sure. Why do you ask?" Melody resumed her place at the table.

"Well," Bethany spoke up. "I was wondering if you needed help."

"Do you sew?" Melody asked.

"Yes, I do. I made all the curtains, blankets…and table coverings," Bethany said, pointing to various linens around the room. She flipped up the edge of the cloth on the dining table so Melody could see her stitching.

"Hmm…" Melody sighed, studying Bethany's stitch work. "Did you sew this by hand?"

"Yes," Bethany said nervously.

"It is very good work. Have you ever worked with a sewing machine?" Melody asked.

"No. But, I'm a fast learner." Bethany was praying that Melody would say yes.

Melody thought a moment. "Why don't you come in with Sadie tomorrow. I will show you the machine and you can try it out. We will discuss it then." Melody carried her dish into the kitchen.

"Okay," Bethany said excitedly.

"Well, ladies…and gentleman," Melody sighed as she put her cloak on. "I must be on my way. I do not want to get lost out here in the middle of the night."

"There's a nice, bright full moon up. Just follow the road south and you'll come right into town." Zane found his voice again.

"Thank you, Mr. Alan. Thank you all for supper. It was delicious." Melody opened the door and stepped onto the porch.

"I'll walk you out," Sadie said.

"Good night, Bethany," Melody called.

"Bye," Bethany called from the kitchen as she and Zane started washing the dishes.

Sadie carried Melody's cloak for her as Melody finished donning her bonnet and gloves. "Thank you, again, for supper. We must do it again." Melody double-checked the little wagon and hopped onto her horse.

"Yes, we must." Sadie smiled at her new friend. "Have a safe ride back into town," Sadie said, waving from the porch.

"Good night," Melody said and off she rode toward town, the wagon clattering along behind.

"Lord," Sadie prayed. "Your will be done in this friendship."

"Amen," Bethany said, coming out onto the porch.

"She's real nice, Beth. I hope she likes my work," Sadie said.

"She said she did. Now leave it be." Bethany put her hand on Sadie's shoulder. "Now…let's go in and have a nice long chat with that brother of yours."

Sadie smiled. "You can. I think I'll sit out here on the swing for a while."

"Fine," Bethany went back inside.

CHAPTER 22

ROAD TO HEALING

Bethany and Zane were finishing up the dishes as Sadie walked in from saying good night to Melody.

"Thank you for the delicious supper, Beth." Sadie patted her on the shoulder and poured a cup of coffee.

"Yes, thanks. It was wonderful!" Zane said, a little too excitedly.

"Well, you're welcome. But, Zane," she teased. "I don't think you were commenting on my cooking."

Sadie and Bethany looked at each other and then started laughing.

"What's so funny?" Zane whined. "I like your cooking…I just…liked your guest more." He smiled. The girls laughed once more.

"Oh, Zane," Sadie breathed. "We don't mean to laugh. It's just been a long time since either one of us has seen you act like that around a lady."

"Who knows," Bethany chimed. "Maybe this is God's doing."

Zane blushed. "Well, I probably should head on home." He grabbed his coat and hat. "Thanks, again."

"Good night," the girls echoed.

As Zane hopped on Flash, he suddenly felt tired. He took his time getting home. Flash was getting on in years, anyway, and he didn't move as fast as he used to. Zane wanted to talk to God about this woman he had met. He didn't want to fall back into his old ways. When he got home, he fell right into bed. He didn't even bother making a fire or getting undressed.

"Lord," he prayed. "Help me to see what's right."

Zane fell into a deep sleep as the last words of his plea to the Father floated off his lips.

✿✿✿✿

That same night, Seth rode home in silence. Mrs. Skinner wasn't sure if he and Sadie had been arguing when they talked earlier that day, but he didn't seem in the right frame of mind. However, she decided not to pry. She didn't want to jeopardize what God may be doing in Seth's life.

When they arrived home, Seth helped her out of the wagon and then unhitched the horses and sent them out to pasture. He then went into the ranch house and found Mrs. Skinner in the kitchen.

"I'm not coming in for supper, Nanna. I'll have a biscuit or something in the bunkhouse." He walked over to the pantry and pulled out a small bowl of butter.

"Is everything okay, son?" Mrs. Skinner asked, touching Seth's shoulder ever so slightly.

"I'll be okay, Nanna; as soon as I talk to God about it." Seth gave her a kiss on the cheek and bid her a good night.

As he walked back to the bunkhouse, he could think of nothing but that old feeling of wanted desire he used to get whenever he thought of Sadie.

"Lord," he prayed as he entered the bunkhouse. "Clear my mind of all unclean thoughts. I don't want to be the evil thing I was before..." Seth prayed on his knees for a good hour. When he felt he had exhausted God's ear, he opened his Bible to the Psalms. The Psalms always comforted Seth. He didn't quite understand why. Maybe it was because he felt he identified so much with King David.

Seth opened to his favorite Psalm for times like these; Psalm 111. His favorite verse was verse ten where it reads, *'The fear of the Lord is the beginning of wisdom: A good understanding have all they that do his commandments: his praise endureth forever'*.

"Lord," he prayed. "I will try to keep your commandments. I pray for your strength to follow your ways in the times of temptation. Amen!"

Seth then closed his Bible and went to bed.

✡ ✡ ✡ ✡

In the middle of the night, both Zane and Seth were awakened by the same sound; a gunshot. Both men never remembered anything about the nightmare except for that horrible sound.

On this night, however, when they heard the shot they both saw Sadie's face before them. They didn't know what it meant, but Zane couldn't sleep for the rest of the night. Seth prayed for guidance and fell back to sleep.

CHAPTER 23

DAY OF RECONCILIATION

Bethany woke before dawn, too nervous to sleep any longer. She went about her daily chores in a dreamy, mechanical fashion. All she could think about was Seth's piercing gaze and Sadie's past. She liked Seth more and more each day and, from what little she had spoken to him, he seemed repentant. But she couldn't seem to shake the fear she felt for her future…and Sadie's. She was so involved in her thoughts as she mucked out the stalls in the barn that she didn't hear Sadie approaching.

"Good morning!" Sadie greeted cheerfully.

"AAAGH!" Bethany screamed and, as a reflex action, threw the shovel across the stall.

Sadie was laughing so hard that she had to sit down. "I'm sorry," she choked. "I didn't mean to startle you." She giggled and then took some deep breaths to compose herself.

Bethany still held her hand on her heart, trying to calm her hyperventilating. Then she smiled. "That's okay," Bethany breathed. "I needed to be awakened from my daydream."

"What were you dreaming about?" Sadie asked, picking up the shovel and continuing where Bethany had left off.

"Oh…nothing," Bethany said, blushing. "What would you like for breakfast?"

"Hey, it's my turn to cook!" Sadie whined.

"That's okay. You're cooking supper anyway." Bethany smiled. "I'll surprise you," she said, returning to the house… and to her daydreaming.

✡✡✡✡

Seth woke as the cock crowed. He thought he would be tired, but he felt totally refreshed; and famished.

"Why am I so hungry?" he asked himself. Then he remembered that he'd never gotten around to eating anything the night before. He got out of bed and had finished his morning chores in about an hour's time. He then went into the ranch house, heading directly for the kitchen. There wasn't a sound anywhere in the house and the kitchen oven was stone-cold.

"Hmm…she must be sleeping in," he mumbled. He decided to surprise Mrs. Skinner with breakfast.

He put a pot of coffee on the stove after he got a good fire started. Then he went all out. He prepared biscuits and gravy, scrambled eggs, sausage patties (his specialty), and cut up a few apples, sprinkling them with cinnamon sugar. He then pressed some fresh apple juice from a small table top hand press Mrs. Skinner had in the shed out back. Hearing some slight creaking and shuffling above his head, he realized that Mrs. Skinner must be awake. He quickly set the table, placing a pretty daisy at Mrs. Skinner's place. He was placing the last of food on the table as Mrs. Skinner entered the room.

"Good morning!" Seth greeted cheerfully. "I hope you don't mind; I took the liberty," he said, pointing to the food.

"Oh my! No, Seth…I don't mind at all. I'm just sorry I wasn't up to make it for you," she said, yawning.

They both sat down and said grace. As they dished up their food, Seth studied Mrs. Skinner's face a bit. She was a little pale and there were dark circles under her eyes.

"Are you feeling all right, Nanna?" he asked with concern.

"Oh, yes." She smiled. "I just had a long night is all."

"Something I can help you with?" he asked with a full mouth.

"No. I was just prayin'." She continued to eat and Seth felt like the subject was closed.

They ate in silence for a while; each deep in their own thoughts.

"Do you know much… about knowing what dreams might mean?" Mrs. Skinner asked Seth.

"Not really…why?" he asked curiously.

"I had this kinda' odd dream last night. It had you and Sadie…and Zane and Bethany…and that new girl, Melody, all wrapped up in it." Mrs. Skinner was clearing the table as she spoke.

"What was it about?" Seth asked, attentive to Mrs. Skinner's every word.

"Well…I only remember a couple parts." Mrs. Skinner thought for a moment. "You were all here and it was dusk."

"Were we outside or inside?" Seth was feeling nervous, but he didn't know why.

"Um…you were standing on the porch of the ranch house…and the ladies were half-way between the wagon and the front porch." Mrs. Skinner was washing dishes now; mindlessly scrubbing the same pot as she remembered and recounted her dream for Seth.

"Where was Zane?" Seth asked quietly.

"Between you and the girls." Mrs. Skinner was quiet for a moment. "The next thing I remember is waking up to a gunshot."

"I woke up last night to a gunshot, too. But, that's all I remember about it." Seth was fixing a cup of coffee. "I don't know what to make of it."

"Me, neither, my boy." Mrs. Skinner put away the last dish and refilled her coffee from the pot still lightly steaming on the stove. "Why don't we stop off and see the reverend on the way into town?"

"Good idea. I'll go hitch up the horses." Seth was uncertain of this dream, but he had a feeling it had something to do with his future.

Zane woke up around nine in the morning. After that horrifying nightmare, he finally fell into a fitful slumber around four in the morning. He rubbed his eyes, trying to make them focus. He knew it was Saturday, but it didn't feel like it. Tomorrow he would be going to church for the first time in almost thirteen years. He was excited, yet a little apprehensive. Zane didn't know if the townsfolk would accept him. He couldn't help feeling like something was going to happen tomorrow that would certainly change his life…forever.

Zane rode into town after the morning chores were finished. He didn't realize that he hadn't eaten until he had nearly reached the Silver Streak.

"Mornin', Henry!" Zane greeted as he walked up to the bar.

"Howdy, Zane!" Henry seemed a little more cheerful than usual.

"What's up?" Zane asked.

"I just finished drawing up the plans for the kitchen. You wanna' see 'em?" Henry ran back to Zane's office without waiting for a reply.

When he came back, he slapped some sketches down in front of Zane.

"Wow! You've been busy," Zane remarked. He looked over the plans. "These look great!"

"Thanks! I was thinking of buildin' one of them fancy east coast kitchens with the big oven and a cutting block right in the center." Henry's eyes were beaming. "In fact…if you don't mind, I was going to convert the bar here into a cutting block and wash center."

"So, you're gonna' build it here?" Zane asked, pointing to the bar area.

"Yeah…what do ya think?" Henry's smile was fading.

"I think that's a great idea!" Zane beamed.

"You do?" Henry didn't know if he should believe him or not.

"Yes. I was trying to figure out a way to get rid of the bar anyway. We're not going to need it since we won't be sellin' liquor." Zane patted the oak bar and walked over to a table to sit down. "We should figure out how to decorate the rest."

"I thought your sister was gonna' do that?" Henry came and sat down with his drawing pad.

"She is...but I have to give her some ideas." Zane took off his hat and scratched his head. "I don't know where to start."

"Have you eaten yet?" Henry asked.

"No. Why?" Zane felt his stomach turning in knots from hunger.

"Why don't you come over to my place? I'll have Ida cook us up some late breakfast." Henry patted Zane on the shoulder and got up to leave.

"I don't know how Ida put up with you spendin' the night at the saloon so much. She must be really patient." Zane hopped on Flash.

"Yeah...she's a real special person." Henry smiled at the thought of his loving wife.

Zane and Henry rode off without knowing that they were being watched.

✪ ✪ ✪ ✪

Melody's heart skipped a beat as she watched Zane and his friend ride off. She was afraid to admit that she might be falling for Sadie's handsome brother. She turned from the window and continued scrubbing the hard-wood floor. She was so excited to be on her way to full independence. Although she was glad not to be living with her parents anymore, she missed them. It was going to be especially hard once the holidays came, but...she would cross that bridge when she came to it. She hummed her favorite hymn to take her mind off unpleasant memories until Sadie and Bethany arrived.

✡✡✡✡

As she finished her breakfast, Bethany once again drifted into a daydream. All she could see were Seth's piercing ocean blue eyes… and all she could hear was a gunshot.

"Bethany?" Sadie tried to shake her friend out of it. "BETHANY!"

"Huh? What?" Bethany stammered, recovering from the fear that her dream had brought upon her.

"What is with you?" Sadie asked, clearing the table.

"I don't know. I keep seeing Seth's face," Bethany wasn't smiling, but Sadie was. "And I keep hearing a gunshot." She paused. "Sadie, are you all right?" she said, rising to her friend's side.

"Did you say…gunshot?" Sadie asked, almost in a whisper.

"Yes." Bethany helped Sadie to the nearest chair. "What's wrong?"

"I woke up last night… to the sound of a gunshot. Do you think it means anything?" Sadie was starting to regain some color in her cheeks.

"I don't know…maybe we should pray about it." Bethany pulled up a chair right next to Sadie.

They prayed for several minutes, but Sadie just kept feeling worse. She kept thinking that the gunshot was meant for her. *Lord, help me*, she prayed silently.

"Let's just go to town. Maybe the fresh air will bring me to my senses." Sadie got up and went straight for her coat and riding gear.

Bethany caught up to her outside and they both rode off for town. When they arrived at Melody's shop, Sadie had managed to focus her mind on the task at hand; decorating the tailor shop.

They stepped up to the door and knocked.

"Come in!" Melody called, still on her hands and knees, scrubbing the floor.

Bethany entered first. "Morning, Melody!"

"Howdy, Bethany." Melody had been practicing a few key western words so she would fit in better. "How are you?"

"Fine, thank you." Bethany noticed a funny looking machine in the left corner. "Is that the sewing machine?"

Melody noticed Bethany's nervous look. "Don't worry," she said, smiling. "It's much easier than it looks."

Melody led Bethany to the machine and gave her a piece of paper with instructions on it. "Just follow these instructions step by step and you won't fail." Melody left Bethany to her task so she could greet Sadie.

"Hello, Sadie," she said as Sadie finally stepped inside.

"Howdy, Melody. Do you have any ideas yet?" Sadie asked, getting right to it.

"Boy, you do not mince words, do you?" Melody smiled. "I have a few ideas, but I have a gift for you first."

"A gift? Whatever for?" Sadie asked in shock.

Melody walked over to an easel in the right corner and uncovered it. It read 'SADIE ALAN'S INTERIOR DECORATING'.

Sadie gasped with delight. "Oh, Melody! It's wonderful! But…I'll never fit this thing in my room," she said, pointing to the easel.

"It's not going in your room," Melody said confidently.

"What?" Sadie was confused.

"I want you to share my shop." Melody smiled.

"Really?" Sadie squealed with delight.

"I have already sent for the marquise sign with both of our names on it. It should arrive within the month." Melody could tell Sadie was excited to the point of tears and she thought her heart would burst with delight.

"Now, how are you doing, Miss Bethany?" Melody asked.

"I think I have it. Here," Bethany said, handing the fabric to Melody.

Melody inspected it very closely. "Hmm...you seem to be a natural. Here," she said, handing it back. "This is for you."

Bethany opened it and noticed it was an apron. There were some words embroidered on the front. "Mel's Tailor Shop," Bethany read. "You mean...I'm hired?"

"Yes, ma'am. How does Monday sound for your first day?" Melody was smiling so hard she thought her face would crack.

"Oh, thank you, Melody!" Bethany hugged her and then showed her apron to Sadie.

"Now we can all be together," Melody said quietly. "I must admit...I felt very at home in your company. I hope we become great friends."

Bethany and Sadie nodded to each other and then hugged Melody.

"I hope we do, too, Mel," Bethany said.

"Well...I don't mean to be rude, but I have to buy some groceries and get home. We're having a guest for dinner." Sadie tugged on Bethany's blouse. "Are you coming, Beth?"

"Yes. Thank you, again, Melody." Bethany folded her apron.

"No...*thank you*," Melody replied.

They waved good bye and walked down to the mercantile.

✿✿✿✿

Seth went out to sweep the front porch once he saw Zane ride off. His mind was wandering to past times; remembering the hate that had shone from Zane's eyes when he knew that Seth was the one who violated his sister. Seth had never seen so much hate. He wondered if Zane's heart

153

still bore him ill will. Seth was so deep in thought, he didn't hear the girls approach.

"Hello, Seth," Sadie called as she approached.

"Mornin' ladies," he said, snapping out of his daydream. "Can I help you find something?"

"We're just shopping for tonight," Bethany said. "Is there anything you don't like to eat?"

"Oh, I'm pretty easy to please," he said with a wink.

Bethany blushed and walked inside. Sadie was smiling and trying to hold back a giggle or two. She wanted Bethany and Seth's relationship to blossom. She didn't know that Seth still harbored some feelings for her.

"Have you been praying?" Seth asked Sadie.

"About...?" She wasn't really paying attention.

"About our conversation tonight." Seth could tell he wasn't getting a full audience.

"Yes, I have." Sadie didn't want anything to sway her mood right now.

"So have I. There are many things I have to tell you, Sadie, I don't want these things to become a wedge between us. Please pray before our little talk." Seth was pleading she would do as he asked.

"Of course, I will. But, I want you to pray, too. I believe God's wanting you to come over for more than just reconciliation between you and me." Sadie was serious now.

"What do you mean?" Seth didn't know what Sadie was trying to say.

"I believe the Lord wants you to consider courting Bethany," Sadie whispered.

Seth was dumbfounded. He never would have guessed in a million years that's what Sadie was trying to tell him. He remembered the first day he'd met Bethany. He also remembered being attracted to her, but he thought that was just a physical attraction; so he put it out of his mind.

Sadie walked inside, satisfied she had stimulated his brain to think about the situation at hand. She and Bethany shopped for the items they needed and Mrs. Skinner checked them out. All the while, Seth sat on the bench in front of the store.

As they were walking out, Bethany stopped. "I forgot something," she said, and walked back inside. Sadie waited for her at the end of the porch as she eyed Seth out of the corner of her eye. He looked like he was praying. Bethany came out a few moments later with a wrapped package under her arm.

"What do you have there?" Sadie asked with a twinkle in her eye.

"Nothing important." Bethany just started walking back to the livery.

"Hey, wait for me," Sadie said, trying to catch up.

They got on their horses and rode home in silence; each consumed with their own thoughts.

✡ ✡ ✡ ✡

Zane and Henry drew up several different ideas and plans for the hotel for the remainder of the day. Zane wanted to match the inside with the name, 'The Silver Streak'. He wanted a lot of silver, but he didn't know what colors to coordinate it with.

"I'm no good at this stuff," he said, throwing his pencil down in frustration.

"Sure you are," Henry consoled. "Look at what you've done so far."

"I haven't done much," Zane said, feeling defeated. "I think I'll stop by my sister's on the way home and get her ideas."

"Good idea," Henry said, sighing. "Want to stay for supper?"

"I've already inconvenienced you enough," Zane protested.

"Nonsense," Ida, Henry's wife, said. "You'll always be considered family, Zane Alan, now you're stayin' and that's that."

"Yes, ma'am," he chuckled.

✰✰✰✰

Bethany went straight up to her room when she and Sadie arrived home. She took the wrapped package with her and didn't come down until right before Seth was supposed to arrive. As Bethany walked down the stairs, all Sadie could do was to stare. She had never seen Bethany so dressed up; not even for church.

"Wow!" Sadie whispered in awe.

"Do you like it?" Bethany asked, straitening the folds of her new emerald green gown.

"Oh, yes. It really makes your eyes stand out." Sadie looked at Bethany's hair. "I like your hair up. It shows off the lovely shape of your face."

"Thank you," she said, patting her curls; piled high on her head with one lone curl draped over her right shoulder.

Then they heard a knock. "I'll get it," Bethany said, trying to calm her nerves.

She walked to the door and took a deep breath. Then, with cheeks flushed, she opened the door. She held her breath at the sight of their guest. Seth was dressed in a black suit, complete with vest and hat. His boots were shined so that you could see your reflection. His hair was slicked back and his eyes were bright as the setting sun.

"Hello, Mr. Gates. Won't you come in?" Bethany opened the door wide to let him in.

"Thank you," he said, entering slowly.

"Howdy, Seth," Sadie said cheerfully.

"Hello, Sadie." Seth was more nervous about his talk with her than being with Bethany.

"Uh…may I take your coat?" Bethany asked, clearing her throat.

Seth handed her his hat and suit jacket. Then he handed Bethany a gift.

"Flowers! How beautiful!" Bethany took them and held them like they were a newborn babe. "Thank you, Seth."

"You're very welcome," he said quietly.

"Well, supper is almost ready. Why don't you two fix a cup of coffee and have a seat in the living room. I'll call when the meal is ready." Sadie winked at Bethany and handed her a tray of coffee and appetizers of fruit and honey rolls.

Seth and Bethany sat on the davenport in the living room and sipped coffee for a few minutes before either spoke.

"You look lovely," Seth said quietly.

"Thank you. You're looking pretty dapper, yourself." Bethany was remembering the first day they met. She felt so at ease talking to him then.

"Thank you." Seth took a sip of coffee. "Um…how is the work hunting going?"

"Fine. I start at the tailor shop on Monday." Bethany took a sip of coffee and then set her cup down. "Melody is really starting to relax. I think she really likes our little town."

"Hmm…" Seth was at a loss for words.

"Supper's ready," Sadie called.

Seth sat at the head of the table. Bethany was on his left and Sadie on his right.

"Seth, would you say the blessing for our meal, please?" Sadie grabbed his hand and reached for Bethany's.

When Seth was finished praying he scooted his chair back from the table. "Um…where is your washroom?" he asked Sadie.

"Upstairs, the last door on your right," Sadie said, pouring water in each person's glass.

"Thank you. Excuse me," he said to Bethany.

Bethany nodded and watched him leave the room.

Sadie giggled. "I didn't realize you liked him that much."

Bethany gave her a glare. "Yes, I like him...very much," she said softly. "But, I think this was the wrong night to be trying to play matchmaker."

"What are you talking about?" Sadie said, acting innocent.

"It's totally obvious his mind is elsewhere," Bethany said, emphasizing the last word with flare.

"Yeah," Sadie said, sobering. "I hope God will change that by the end of the evening."

"Why?" Bethany asked.

Sadie didn't answer as Seth had just returned to the table.

"You didn't have to wait for me." Seth looked embarrassed.

"That's okay," Sadie said, dishing up her plate.

"Sadie, have you forgotten your manners?" Bethany hissed. "Guests are served first."

"Oops," Sadie said, blushing. "Help yourself, Seth."

They all ate in silence except for a few compliments on the food. When it came time for dessert, Bethany got up from the table.

"I'll clear the table," Bethany said. "Why don't you two go into the living room and I'll bring you dessert and coffee in there."

"Are you sure, Beth?" Sadie asked. "I wouldn't want you to get anything on your new dress."

"I'll be all right," she replied. "That's what aprons are for. Now, go on." She shooed them away as she began to clear the dishes.

Seth sat in the chair in the far corner and Sadie sat on the davenport. There were no words exchanged for each was waiting for the prompting of the Holy Spirit before they began.

A few minutes later, Bethany brought a tray of coffee and tarts and set it on the table by the chair where Seth was sitting.

"I'm going to go up and change and then do the dishes," she said as she retreated.

"Beth?" Sadie called.

Bethany turned and faced her friend, smiling.

"Thank you," Sadie said quietly.

"Sure thing," Bethany said, walking slowly up the stairs.

"She's a great friend," Seth commented.

"Yes, she is," Sadie whispered, taking a sip of coffee. "Why don't…we pray first."

"Good idea," Seth said, bowing his head.

"Lord," Sadie started, "please guide our words and steps as we finish what was started so many years ago."

"And Father," Seth finished, "may your will be done this evening as we reach a goal of reconciliation and renewed friendship."

"Amen," they echoed.

Seth took a deep breath and grabbed his Bible, which lay on the coffee table.

Sadie reached for her Bible and opened briefly to a page in the back. She pulled out a piece of paper and closed the Book once more. They heard Bethany rattling around in the kitchen and both sighed at the same time.

"First," Seth spoke, clearing his throat. "I want to explain a little why I did what I did." He cleared his throat once more and took a deep breath. "Um…you knew I had a big crush on you, right?"

Sadie nodded, looking at the floor.

"Well…I was being so rebellious at home that I did anything I could to embarrass my father. He and I never really got along. Any positive attitude and thinking went into impressing you. I got so hung up on the effort of getting your attention that it became an obsession." Seth had to pause to take another deep breath. "When you told me you wouldn't go out with me…it intensified my obsession." One lone tear trailed down his cheek. "I felt that if…I couldn't have you… nobody should." Seth ran his hands over his face and took a deep breath. "I am…so sorry, Sadie," he choked out. "I wish to *God* I could give back what I stole from you."

Sadie was trying very hard not to lose her composure. She could feel a weight lift from her shoulders she never realized was there. She felt the Holy Spirit's presence. She walked over to where Seth was sitting and knelt in front of him. He wouldn't look at Sadie. He kept his gaze on his clenched fists that lay on top of his Bible in his lap.

"Seth," Sadie whispered. "I forgive you."

Surprised, he looked up into her eyes; his own wide with anxiety. "You do?"

"Yes…I do. I forgave you years ago. And," she got up and sat in the chair next to him, "so did the Lord."

Seth took some long, deep breaths in order to compose himself. "I know God has forgiven me…and I guess I believe you've forgiven me, too." He wiped his brow on his shirtsleeve. "I think the problem I have is forgiving myself."

Sadie picked up her Bible and sat back down next to Seth. "It says here in…" she said, flipping pages open to the Psalms. "…Psalms, chapter nine and verse nine, '*The Lord also will be a refuge for the oppressed, a refuge in times of trouble.*' All you have to do is give your guilt to the Lord and he'll free you."

"Would you pray for me?" Seth asked quietly.

"Certainly," Sadie said, taking his hand and bowing her head.

Bethany knelt at the kitchen table and quietly prayed for Seth, as well. She then rose and walked out back and around the side of the house to the rose garden. She was picking the last few roses left when she heard a horse ride up. Peeking around the front of the house, she saw Zane sliding off his steed.

CHAPTER 24

ELEMENT OF SURPRISE

Zane rode up to Bethany's house on his way home from supper at Henry and Ida's. He was in turmoil over what to do and say the next day at church if someone started something. So many people around town would have questions about why the saloon was closing and all…He was familiar with many of these "Sunday morning" people from the Friday nights they spent around a poker table. He was also frustrated at his plans for decorating the hotel, so he was eager to talk, and maybe pray, with Sadie.

He wasn't paying much attention when he arrived at the house, so he didn't notice the strange horse out front. Neither did he see Bethany hiding around the side of the house. He stepped off his horse and walked up the front steps. He knocked and waited.

✧ ✧ ✧ ✧

Sadie and Seth were just finishing praying when Bethany ran into the room out of breath.

"Beth, what's wrong?" Sadie asked with concern.

Bethany huffed and puffed, trying to calm down. "Zane…" She couldn't finish for she was too flustered and out of breath.

"What *about* Zane?" Seth asked. Then they heard a knock at the door.

Wide-eyed, Bethany pointed to the door and whispered, "He's here."

A look of horror flashed over Sadie's face as Seth went pale.

"What do we do?" Sadie whispered, clutching Seth's arm.

"I'll be right there!" Bethany called to the visitor at the door.

"I'll hide upstairs." Seth thought a moment. "Is there a back stairway?"

"Yes," Bethany said with her hand on the door.

"Sadie," Zane called through the door. "It's me. Let me in, please? I need to talk to you about tomorrow."

"Just a minute, Zane!" Sadie was real nervous.

"I'll go upstairs and if it looks like he's staying for a while, I'll leave out the back." Seth picked up his coat and hat. "Thank you for the meal…and your prayers."

"You're welcome," Sadie and Bethany echoed as they watched Seth retreat up the staircase.

When they felt the coast was clear, Sadie went into the kitchen to put on a fresh pot of coffee and Bethany opened the door.

"Sorry to keep you waiting, Zane," she said quietly. "We were…praying."

"Oh…I'm sorry. Should I come back later?" Zane asked, truly embarrassed.

"NO!" Bethany said a little too loudly. "Please come in. Have a seat in the living room and I'll bring out some coffee."

"Thanks," Zane said as he sat in the chair that only moments ago held Seth.

Seth sat at the top of the stairs praying. He felt an urge to present himself to the one person he hadn't apologized to, but he didn't know if it was the Lord's will. He also prayed that Zane's hate had dissolved and Sadie would have the right words to say.

Bethany brought out a tray of cookies and Sadie followed with a pot of coffee. They set their trays down on the coffee table.

"So…what's on your mind, Zane?" Bethany asked quietly.

He didn't answer right away. He sat there staring into his cup of coffee.

"Is everything all right?" Sadie asked Zane pensively.

"I don't know." Zane thought a moment. "I'm scared about tomorrow, Sadie."

"What are you afraid of?" Sadie was wondering if Seth had left yet.

"What if they don't believe me," Zane whined. "Right now...*I* don't even believe me."

"What are you talking about, Zane?" Bethany was closest to the stairwell and didn't hear a sound. She thought Seth had left.

"I've just been wonderin' lately what I would do if *he* ever showed up." Zane was struggling with anger; anger deep down inside from old wounds not completely healed yet.

"You mean...Seth?" Sadie asked quietly, placing her hand on Zane's.

"How can you say his name so...so...calm and sweet?" Zane replied sarcastically. "He's a thief, Sadie. He stole something from you that you won't ever get back."

"I know that," Sadie cut in, a little too loudly. "But...I've forgiven him, Zane."

"How?" Zane looked defeated.

"Well...first you have to accept God's forgiveness. You did that when you asked Jesus to be your savior." Sadie smiled at her big brother. He looked so vulnerable.

Seth remained frozen to the top of the stairs, silently praying... feeling panicky and confused.

"What do I do next?" Zane felt like his heart would break in two.

"Then you need to forgive yourself," Bethany said. "You won't be able to forgive Seth until you do that."

"That's harder than it sounds," Zane said, staring at the floor.

"It *is* hard," Sadie sighed. "But, if you remember to give God control over the situation...it'll happen."

Zane sat there for the longest moment, thinking about his life and what it had amounted to. "Would you pray for me, Sadie? I don't want to be… like Pa… anymore."

"Certainly," Sadie said, taking both of Zane's hands in hers. "Heavenly Father…"

They prayed for a good five minutes; all the while Seth sat at the top of the stairs listening and praying. He felt what he believed to be the Holy Spirit nudging him to go down and talk to Zane, but he was afraid; afraid of the pending anger and hate Zane may still be holding against him.

"Lord," Seth whispered, "give me strength to do your will."

When Zane and Sadie had finished praying, Bethany refilled the coffee mugs and Sadie continued the conversation.

"Well…" Zane walked over to where his saddlebags were hanging and pulled out his sketches. "Henry and I have been making sketches of our ideas for decoratin', but I want your opinion."

"Wow," Sadie exclaimed, looking over the plans. "You've been busy."

"I'm stuck on how to put it all together. I mean, we have colors and fabrics picked, but…" Zane stammered.

"You can't see the final picture?" Sadie smiled at her big brother.

"Yeah…what do I do next?" Zane was completely unaware of the person who had quietly tiptoed down the stairs and now stood a few feet behind him.

"Can I help?" Seth asked in a cheerful, booming voice.

Everyone jumped and the girls gasped with surprise. They all were not expecting Seth to be there.

"Seth, what are you doing?" Bethany said, tugging at his shirt sleeve and pulling him toward the front door. "You need to leave."

"I'm following God's will," Seth said, yanking his sleeve from Bethany's grip.

Zane stood slowly and stared long and hard at Seth. He truly didn't know what to say. He could feel his old nature creeping up on him, though. Slowly the anger grew until he felt he would explode. He forgot the conversation and prayer time he just had with Sadie and Bethany. He forgot everything that had happened to him in the last two weeks. All he could remember was the anger, hurt and feelings of betrayal he felt when the moment was fresh and new twelve years prior.

Sadie was frightened for her brother and for Seth. She watched Zane intently, noticing the red line of anger rising in his face.

Bethany knelt in a corner by the staircase and prayed.

Seth was frozen in time. He felt total peace in his spirit and knew God would protect him. He just stared at Zane with all the love he had left.

"Hello, Zane," Seth said quietly, his eyes falling to the floor.

"What…in the Sam Hill…are *you* doing here?!" Zane spat through clenched teeth. He could feel a war going on inside his heart. It felt like his old nature was winning.

"Asking… for your forgiveness." Seth glowed with the peace of the Holy Spirit. "I need to ask you for your forgiveness for violating your sister and I need to tell you…I'm very sorry for betraying you and your family."

Zane was dumbfounded. He never expected Seth to stand so confident and yet so humble and admit he was wrong. It put a dent in the wall of hate Zane had once again erected around his heart, but…the wall did not fall.

"You're sorry?" Zane repeated with a flare of sarcasm. His hands began to shake; not from the anger, but from a fear of what he would do to Seth if he remained here any longer. "NO! I will not forgive you!" he screamed as he picked up his hat and saddlebags. "Sadie, tell me one thing?"

"Yes?" she squeaked.

"Did you know he was here?" Zane huffed with angry, jagged breaths.

"Yes, I did," she said, resigning to God's will; whatever it may be.

"Then I wash my hands of you," Zane said, storming out the front door. He wanted to take it back, but he didn't know how.

Sadie ran outside. "Zane, wait!" she called. "What about church tomorrow?"

"To blazes with church!" Zane yelled as he sped off on Flash towards his home.

Bethany and Seth walked out to meet Sadie on the porch. She was sitting in the porch swing, weeping. Bethany knelt beside her and laid her hand on Sadie's knee. "It's okay, Sadie," she said gently. "The Lord will lead him back."

Sadie hugged Bethany real hard and then walked over to where Seth was standing at the opposite end of the porch.

"Why did you do that?" she whispered.

"I sat at the top of the stairs the whole time and prayed," Seth explained. "I felt that the Lord wanted me to present myself, but I was afraid; until you started praying with Zane."

"What happened then?" Sadie's own anger was dissipating.

"I felt all the tension in my spirit just fade away. When that happened...I felt released to come down." Seth frowned and asked for strength to keep his composure. "But...I'm afraid my timing was off."

Sadie took a deep breath and let it out slow. She touched Seth's shoulder lightly and it looked like he was trying to hold on to his emotions but it wasn't working.

"It's not your fault, Seth," she said loud enough for him to hear.

He jumped a little and quickly tried to regain his composure.

"I...didn't know you...were still here," he said, wiping his eyes on his shirt sleeve.

"It's okay," she said, moving towards the front door. "Would you like to have a cup of coffee and talk a little before you head home?" They walked inside and discussed the matter over coffee until the late hours of the evening. Each tried to reassure the others that things would work out... although each truly doubted their own words.

CHAPTER 25

FITS OF RAGE

Zane was blinded by a measure of fury that he hadn't felt in a very long time. When he left Bethany's house, he started toward home, overworking his old horse all the way. "I've got to get away," he hissed through clenched teeth as the wind whipped his long hair into a tangled weave.

When he reached his home, he dismounted before Flash had come to a full stop, a cloud of dust staining the moonlight. He kicked open the front door and picked up the first breakable thing that his eyes fell upon; his mamma's favorite vase. With all the strength he felt he had left, he hurled the vase across the room where it crashed against the hearth of the fireplace. Grabbing a fist full of hair and pulling as hard as he could, he let out a blood-curdling scream.

He burst through the back door and out into the field behind the house. He ran until it felt like his lungs would burst. He finally stopped at the top of a small grassy knoll and just fell to his knees, heaving for air and ignoring the wetness on his cheeks. All the anger, all the hurt, all the old wounds were bleeding inside of him once again. He let all he had left just drain away into the fading twilight. He felt empty of all emotion. Where was God in times like this? His rage made him forget all that he had learned in the past few days. Zane sat on the knoll until the sun slipped down beneath the horizon and then he walked back to the house.

As he neared the house, he heard Flash neighing out front and realized he had forgotten about his trusty steed. He walked the horse to the barn, removed his saddle and gave him a good, long rub down… perhaps a bit too roughly.

"I'm sorry, boy," Zane sighed. "I didn't mean to take it out on you."

You need to take it out on Seth, a little voice teased.

Zane knew he was different now than he used to be, but he couldn't control his anger when he saw Seth.

He deserves to suffer for what he did to your sister.

Zane kept hearing his old nature arguing with what he knew was growing in his heart; love.

"I don't know what to do," Zane said, sitting on the milking stool.

LISTEN TO MY VOICE, MY SON.

"Who was that?" Zane said, startled from what sounded like an audible voice. He looked around the barn and outside, but nobody was there. Puzzled, Zane walked back to the house and sat in his favorite chair, surveying the mess he had made of one of the only treasures left that had belonged to his mother. He stared into the fire for a long time, not thinking of anything.

MY SON.

Zane jumped out of his chair, "Who was that?!" He was getting upset now. After a minute of silence, he sat back down. He closed his eyes and thought of the events of the evening.

How dare Sadie keep this from me! Zane thought. *How could she just go and forgive him like that?*

THROUGH ME, MY SON.

Zane was used to the voice now. He knew it had to be God speaking to his heart, but...*I don't know what to believe anymore*, he thought, staring at his Bible on the table.

He slowly scanned the room. His eye caught something shimmering in the firelight. There...on the top shelf of the kitchen hutch; something mostly hidden behind old cans and jars. Zane got up from his chair and reached for the shimmering object. When he moved the cans and jars out of the way he saw the object of his interest; a bottle of whiskey. For a long moment, he just stared at it. He slowly reached for the bottle with a trembling hand. Holding it in one hand he steadied himself with the other.

Drink it, Zane. There was that teasing voice again.

Zane licked his lips as beads of sweat glistened on his forehead. He walked back to his chair and sat down; the bottle of whiskey stuck in his hands.

Drink it, Zane. Who would it hurt?

Zane's anger slowly returned as the teasing voice continued to whisper bitter sweet nothings to his mind.

Come on, Zane. You know you've missed it.

"Yes, I have," Zane said with shaken confidence.

You deserve it after today. You need it.

"Yes...I do," Zane hissed through clenched teeth. He uncorked the bottle and raised it near his nose. He inhaled and let it out in a low sigh.

Drink it.

As Zane raised the bottle to his lips, he hesitated.

RESIST, MY SON.

"I can't," he whispered as he inhaled the smoky liquid.

At first, Zane's tongue stung with the taste of the evil drink. But he drank it slowly and got more used to it with every swallow. He relaxed into his chair and let his anger bubble to the top. By morning, he was more drunk than he had ever been and madder than a rabid dog. In his drunkenness, he vaguely remembered something about church. It was Sunday and all his loved ones...and enemies...would be at church right now. He mustered up the strength he needed to walk, picked up his gun and saddled Flash.

"I'll show 'em," he slurred to the wind and headed out for town.

✮✮✮✮

Bethany, Seth and Sadie sat in the front pew as Reverend Cochran preached a powerful sermon. At least it sounded powerful with the Reverend pounding on the podium to emphasize each point. But none of the three were paying any attention to the Reverend. They were all worried what Zane might do to himself...or them. They had no idea what God had planned in all of this. Sadie was silently praying that the good Lord would speak to Zane's tender heart and protect him from the temptations of anger and hatred.

As the service ended, Bethany and Sadie stood talking to Melody in the back of the church sanctuary. Seth was in the Reverend's office waiting for him to finish greeting his parishioners.

"Mornin', Seth," Reverend Cochran bellowed as he walked behind his desk and sat down.

"Howdy, Reverend," Seth chimed. He tried not to let on that there was anything wrong.

"What can I do for ya'?" the Reverend asked.

Seth nervously flipped the pages in his Bible. "Um...I need your help...with something."

"Certainly," Reverend said, smiling.

"Well..." Seth hesitated. "I did something last night because I thought God was telling me to."

"Yes?" the reverend prompted.

"Well...the deed had a disastrous outcome and I'm still not sure if I'm going to lose my life over it." Seth folded his hands in his lap to calm his nerves.

Reverend Cochran eyed Seth with a keen sense of discernment. "He saw you, didn't he?" he asked confidently.

"Yeah...at Bethany's house." Seth lowered his gaze to the worn Bible on Reverend Cochran's desk.

The Reverend whistled. "What happened and how did it start?"

Seth went on to explain in great detail the events of the prior evening. "So...what do I do now?"

"Seth, sometimes God's will provokes a hostile reaction."

"Uh...I don't follow," Seth said intently.

"Zane's wounds are probably still fresh so when he saw you, the wall to protect those wounds immediately went up. He probably ran because he didn't know what to do and it frightened him." Reverend Cochran opened his Bible to the First Epistle of Peter. "Let me read you something." Reverend Cochran adjusted his glasses and started. "This is the third chapter of the book of First Peter, startin' at verse thirteen: *And who is he that will harm you, if ye be followers of that which is good? But if ye suffer for righteousness' sake, happy are ye: and be not afraid of their terror, neither be troubled; But sanctify the Lord God in your hearts: and be ready always to give an answer to every man that asketh you a reason of the hope that is in you with meekness and fear: Having a good conscience; that, whereas they speak evil of you, as of evildoers, they may be ashamed that falsely accuse your good conversation in Christ. For it is better, if the will of God be so, that ye suffer for well doing, than for evil doing.* So you see, Seth," he said, looking up from his Bible. "Sometimes doing the Lord's will may seem less 'glorified' then it should be. But…if you allow Him…God's got it all under control. And the outcome will, also, most likely be His will, as well."

"Hmm…that's a lot to think about," Seth said, standing. "Thank you, Reverend. Pray that everything turns out the way God wanted it."

"You bet, my boy," Reverend Cochran said, shaking Seth's hand.

Seth came out of the reverend's office and found Sadie and Bethany waiting on the front steps with Melody McConner. "Hello, ladies," he said, descending the steps.

"Hi, Seth," Bethany said, smiling.

"How would you lovely ladies like to join Nanna and me for an early supper at the ranch?" Seth walked them to their horses.

Sadie and Bethany looked at each other and shrugged their shoulders.

"Um...I better get on home," Melody said, turning to her own horse. "I will see you girls at work tomorrow."

"Miss McConner," Seth called.

"Yes?" she said, turning back towards Seth.

"I meant to include you in that invitation," Seth said, smiling.

"Really?" she said, sheepishly. "I don't want to be a third wheel."

"You wouldn't be a third wheel, Mel," Bethany said. "You would complete the circle."

"Well..." Melody hesitated, not sure if she should extend her heart a little more and make some new friends.

"Come on, Melody. It'll be really nice to have you join us. After all," Sadie said, taking Melody's hand. "You're part of our family now."

Melody blushed and then squeezed Sadie's hand. "Okay," she said.

"What time would you like us there and what can we bring?" Bethany asked Seth, climbing into her saddle.

"How about four o'clock and you can bring the salad and dessert." Seth hopped on his horse.

"We'll be there," Sadie said and they all waved as Seth rode off.

"Hey, Mel," Bethany called. "How about we pick you up at three?"

"See you then," she said and rode off towards town.

Sadie and Bethany remained in front of the church for a bit longer. Sadie stared at the steeple with a feeling of finality. Bethany noticed the look on her face change.

"What's wrong, Sadie?" she asked as she tightened the straps on her stirrups.

"I don't know," she said as they headed home. "I have this strange feeling that this is my last day at church."

"Do you think Zane will try something?" Bethany asked nervously.

"I hope not. I hope the Lord'll just rein in Zane's heart and remind him that he doesn't have to hold onto that hate anymore." Sadie looked around the valley as they rode towards home. The feeling was getting stronger and stronger; the feeling that she was living the last day of her life.

✡ ✡ ✡ ✡

Zane managed to get to town without falling off of Flash. He could feel the effects of the liquor wearing off and his head pounded like a blacksmith pounding on hot steel. He prodded Flash toward the Silver Streak and groggily dismounted. He was glad that Henry wasn't around. He didn't want to feel any more embarrassed than he already did. Shuffling back to his old office, he lifted up a couple of loose floor boards under the back of his desk. There lay two shiny bottles of bourbon: this was where he had always hid the good stuff. He picked one up, uncorked it, and slugged down half the bottle. Replacing the cork, he slid the slender glass bottle into his vest pocket and took it with him. He hopped back on Flash and headed out of town towards the church.

As he approached, he could see that there were only four horses and one carriage left out in front of the church, so he figured it had already let out. When he got closer, he noticed Bethany and his sister standing on the steps. He didn't want them to see him, so he hid behind a small grove of trees at the end of the path that led up to the church from the main road. "I'll wait here," he groaned.

A few minutes later, he noticed a man walk out and start talking with the ladies. "That mus' be him," Zane slurred. He watched as Seth mounted his horse and started off down the path towards where Zane was hiding. He remained very still as Seth rode by and headed in the opposite direction of town. As soon as Zane felt the coast was clear, he slowly rode in the same direction as Seth. He rode for a while, not noticing that Seth was no longer in front of him.

"Musta' turn off," Zane slurred as he took another swig of liquor. He followed the road for a while longer and saw a ranch in the distance. He remembered from a long time ago that the Skinners lived out this way. "Thass' where he is," Zane spat out.

He rode on in silence, stopping once to recheck his gun to make sure it was loaded. When he reached the lane that led to the Skinners', he stopped to survey his situation. He noticed that there was a small grove of evergreens leading all the way up to the back of the ranch house. He decided to dismount and leave his horse tied to a tree by the road. He pulled his gun from its holster, stuck the bottle of courage back in his vest pocket, and headed through the trees towards the ranch house. As soon as he came to a building that looked like a bunkhouse, he hid behind it and waited until Seth came out.

✡ ✡ ✡ ✡

Seth arrived home and did his afternoon chores. He hummed hymns as he went along, not really expecting anything but the ladies arriving later. When he finished, he walked inside the ranch house to look for Mrs. Skinner.

"Nanna?" he called.

"In the kitchen, son," Mrs. Skinner called back.

"I've invited three guests for supper," he said, kissing her on the cheek. "Is that all right?"

"Of course, Seth," she said, continuing to pull the husks off the corn she had in the washbasin. "Who did you invite?"

"Bethany, Sadie and the new lady in town, Miss Melody McConner." Seth dipped his finger lightly into the steaming pot of gravy setting on the back of the stove.

Mrs. Skinner slapped his hand and smiled. "How nice. No male companions?" she teased.

"Nanna," Seth moaned. "They're just friends."

"Mm-Hmm," she sighed as she paced off toward the smoke house to get some more meat.

Seth set the table and put some flowers in a vase in the center of it. He put the biscuits in the oven and shucked the rest of the corn for Mrs. Skinner. He was just finishing rubbing off the silk when she returned with a large, lightly smoked rump roast.

"Why, thank you, Seth," she said, patting him on the cheek. "Now, why don't you go collect some firewood and then wash up before they get here."

"Yes, ma'am," he said smiling.

Seth walked out back and collected a good amount of firewood for the ranch house. Then he selected a few pieces for the bunk house and headed over there to change and wash up.

Zane had fallen asleep behind the bunkhouse, but was awakened by the sound of a door closing. He took another swig of bourbon and inched up to the window to peek in. He saw Seth changing his clothes and washing his face. Zane noticed Seth was dressing up; donning a tie and slicking his hair.

"Mus' be havin' guess'," Zane slurred as he sat back down on the ground to think. "I'll haf' to wait it out"

✪✪✪✪

Bethany and Sadie picked up Melody right on time. They had decided to do the salad and Melody brought the dessert.

"Mmmm…that cobbler smells delicious," Bethany said as Melody climbed in the wagon.

"Thank you," Melody said smiling. "I tried one of your recipes. I hope it turned out okay."

"Oh, I'm sure it did. I can't wait to have some." Bethany was really excited about this afternoon. She would actually be able to sit down to a full meal with Seth this time without being all nervous.

Sadie wasn't really paying attention to Melody's and Bethany's conversation. Her mind kept wandering to past memories of her parents and her brother in happier times. She was remembering her childhood and when she got saved at church.

"Sadie?" Bethany called, shaking Sadie's arm.

"Huh...what?" she said, coming out of her daydream.

"What's wrong?" Melody asked.

Sadie frowned and looked down at the salad she carried in her lap.

"Are you still having those feelings?" Bethany asked.

Sadie nodded as one lone tear fell from her closed eyes. "It's getting stronger and stronger the closer we get to Nanna's."

"What feelings?" Melody asked, wondering what was so stressful for Sadie.

"I keep feeling weird… like it's my last day of life or something," Sadie said quietly.

Bethany pulled the wagon to a stop for a moment. "Do you want to go back?"

"No," Sadie said suddenly. "That would be rude. I'll be okay. I think I just need to eat something." Sadie did her best to reassure her friends that everything was okay.

"Are you sure, Sadie?" Melody asked, gently touching her shoulder.

"Yes. I'm sure," she said smiling. "Now, let's get going. We're going to be late."

Bethany snapped the reins and the wagon jerked into motion once again. When they reached the road to Mrs. Skinner's, all three noticed Flash tied by the side of the road. They all looked at each other with surprise and fear; Bethany snapped the reins to hurry the horses. They rode into Mrs. Skinner's courtyard, stirring up dust as they stopped. Sadie jumped out of the wagon and hastily handed the salad to Melody.

"Seth," Sadie and Bethany called loudly.

Seth came running out of the bunkhouse; shaving foam still covering half of his face.

"What's wrong?" he huffed as he reached them.

"Oh…you're all right," Bethany said, unconsciously touching the clean side of Seth's face.

"Of course, I am. Why would you ask?" he said, brushing her hand away.

"We spotted Zane's horse tied to a tree out at the main road," Sadie said chokingly. "I think he's here."

They all looked around nervously.

"Why don't you ladies go on into the house and I'll join you in a minute," Seth said, waving them on and returning to the bunk house.

Zane had heard every word they'd said. He decided to wait until the ladies were leaving… and surprise them all.

CHAPTER 26

BREATH OF PEACE

Supper passed uneventfully, save for the wonderful fellowship everyone was having around Mrs. Skinner's table. When they had all finished, Sadie and Melody cleared the table and began washing the dishes.

"What can I do?" asked Bethany, rolling up her sleeves.

Sadie looked at Melody and winked then smiled at Bethany. "Nothing," she said with authority.

"What? Nonsense. There's plenty of cleaning up to go around." Bethany pulled a hand towel from a hook on the wall and began drying the clean dishes.

Melody took the dish and towel from Bethany's hands. "We will take care of it. You have more important things to do," she said with a wink.

Bethany blushed. "Are you certain? I wouldn't feel right about leaving all the work for the two of you."

"Yes…we're positive," Sadie said, giving Bethany a playful shove. "Now go."

"Well…the least I can do is take coffee to our hosts." Bethany set to work making a fresh pot of coffee. She set the serving tray with three cups and a small pitcher of cream. Her final touch was a flower plucked from the table centerpiece. As she left the kitchen, she heard her friends whispering and giggling. She smiled and silently thanked the Lord for such wonderful friends.

As Bethany entered the living room, she noticed Seth sitting close to the hearth, staring into the fire. Mrs. Skinner was sitting in a rocker in the center of the room, knitting. Bethany set the serving tray on a small table in front of Mrs. Skinner and poured three cups of coffee.

"What would you like in your coffee, Nanna?" she asked cheerfully.

"Oh, I just drink it black, dear. Thank you," she said, setting her knitting down and taking her cup from Bethany.

Bethany glanced at Seth and hesitated.

"He drinks it black, too," Mrs. Skinner whispered and smiled.

Bethany carried a cup over to the hearth and gently touched Seth's shoulder.

He turned and smiled. "Thank you, Beth," he said, taking the cup from her.

Shivers ran up Bethany's spine as she walked back and retrieved her own cup. She sat down in a chair that was positioned between Seth and Mrs. Skinner.

Nobody said a word for a few minutes. Each was in their own thoughts. The only sounds they heard were Mrs. Skinner's knitting needles clinking and Melody and Sadie talking in the kitchen.

Mrs. Skinner couldn't stand the silence any longer. "Ya'll are so quiet. What's on your minds?"

"Zane," Seth and Bethany said simultaneously.

"What about him?" Mrs. Skinner asked, setting her knitting aside.

Seth explained the events of the night before and told Mrs. Skinner what Reverend Cochran had said.

"Hmm…" Mrs. Skinner sighed. "Is there a chance of danger?"

"Yes," Bethany spoke up. "He's outside somewhere right now."

"How do ya know?" Mrs. Skinner walked to the front window and looked out.

"We saw his horse tied to a tree at the end of your lane as we arrived earlier." Bethany held on to her coffee cup with both hands to hide her trembling.

Mrs. Skinner turned back to her guests. She noticed Melody and Sadie had slipped in and were seated on the couch.

"I think we all need to kneel and pray for the Lord's guidance and protection," Mrs. Skinner announced, grabbing Bethany's hand and kneeling in the center of the room. Everyone knelt in a circle and held hands as Mrs. Skinner began praying.

"Heavenly Father," she paused, "we bow before thee in humbleness, seeking your guidance on this matter. Father, we don't want to be careless and try to fix this problem by ourselves. Guide us and direct us in what we need to do. Help us to know what you want us to do for our brother, Zane. Father, he's new to your fold and we don't wish for him to perish so quickly. Speak to his heart, Lord. Make him see your good and perfect will for his life. Make him see that harming another of your children won't make his hurt go away; it'll only make it worse. In your Son's name," Mrs. Skinner paused for the others to pray.

"Lord," Bethany continued. "Only you know what the outcome of today will be. Help us to accept whatever that outcome will be. Lord, I pray you'd calm our hearts and minds and spirits and help us to see your hand in all of this. Life is such a precious thing. Help us not to take advantage of it."

"Father God," Melody prayed. "I pray that you would surround this ranch with your warring angels. I pray that you would protect us from the evil that may try to corrupt us through this event. And, Father…I pray that you would especially protect Sadie through this whole thing. These feelings of finality she's been having…I pray you would shed some light on their meaning to her. In the name of Jesus…"

"Lord," Seth continued, "I pray that you'd forgive us of our sins of doubt and fear through this whole situation. Help us to remember that you have everything under control. Father…your will be done. In Jesus' name we all pray, amen."

"Amen," they echoed.

When they opened their eyes, Sadie was missing from the circle.

"Where's Sadie?" Bethany asked.

They stood and looked around the room. Sadie wasn't there, so they searched the rest of the house, calling out her name. There was no sign of her.

"Where could she have gone?" Melody asked, concerned.

"I think I'll check outside," Bethany said, heading for the front door. When she walked outside, she saw Sadie talking to Zane over by the bunkhouse. Bethany ran back inside to tell the others. All but Seth came out to see.

"He looks drunk," Mrs. Skinner commented.

"He probably is," Bethany sighed. "I'll walk over and see if he's calmed down any."

She walked slowly over to Sadie's side and stood listening as her dear friend tried to calm her brother down.

"Zane," Sadie pleaded. "You can't go on for the rest of your days hating him. Hate will eat at your soul until there's nothing left. Please put the gun away. Please, Zane?"

"How can you be s' appy, Sadie?" Zane slurred. "He took you innsense 'way."

"I forgave him a long time ago, Zane. The Lord helped me to forgive him. And the Lord wants to help you to forgive him, too." Sadie grabbed Zane's free hand. "Please, Zane. I beg you…give me the gun."

Zane drank from his bottle once more. It was almost empty. He looked at his sister, then at Bethany. Then Zane stared hard at the bottle. "Here," he slurred, handing Sadie the bottle. "I'm drunk 'nough."

Sadie took the bottle and poured the rest out onto the ground. Then she gave the empty bottle to Bethany and held both of Zane's hands.

"The gun, Zane," Bethany said quietly.

Zane shot an angered glare at Bethany. "Who you to butt in? Gettouta here." He swung his arm out to shoo her away and ended up hitting her in the side of the head.

Bethany walked back to the porch rubbing the side of her head softly.

Mrs. Skinner reached out and hugged her. "Are you all right, darlin'?" she asked.

"Yes," Bethany whispered. "I'll be okay." She laid her head on Mrs. Skinner's shoulder and wept quietly; not for her wound, but for Zane's soul.

Sadie still hung onto Zane's hand. "Zane, please listen to me. You'll never be free until you forgive him…and yourself."

"Myself?" he said, burning inside. "What've I done?"

Sadie started to cry. She just stood there and gazed into Zane's chocolate brown eyes, hoping his spirit would connect with hers and remember the flicker of light left in his heart.

Zane couldn't look into his sister's eyes any longer. He pulled his hand free and started for the front porch, his gun waving wildly in the air.

"Where's he?" Zane shouted in a drunken rage.

Nobody would speak for fear of escalating Zane's already heightened anger.

"Zeth!" Zane shouted in a slurred tongue. "Come out, chicken!"

Seth had been watching through the front window the whole time, praying. He felt nailed to the floor even though he wanted to go out and talk to Zane.

"Lord," Seth prayed. "Help me."

"Where's he?" Zane shouted at the women.

"Right here, Zane," Seth said, coming out onto the porch.

The women wouldn't step aside to let him through because they didn't want anything to happen to Seth.

"Let me through, ladies," Seth said with confidence.

Mrs. Skinner stepped aside and then grabbed Seth's arm as he walked through. "Be careful, son."

"The Lord'll protect me, Nanna," he said, kissing her on the cheek.

Seth stopped at the bottom of the steps. "Put the gun down, Zane. I'm sure we can talk this out like men."

The women moved off the porch and joined Sadie by the wagon. They were frightened for Seth…and for Zane.

Mrs. Skinner fell silent when she surveyed the scene. She suddenly remembered her dream she'd had a couple nights ago. Someone was going to lose their life tonight…and she could have prevented it. She knelt where she was and started praying. Bethany and Melody followed suit and joined her. Sadie went cold inside with fear. She, too, remembered the dream she had. Her mind kept repeating, *What if I'm the one…*

"Bethany," Sadie said, tapping her on the shoulder.

"What is it, Sadie?" Bethany said with concern. She noticed Sadie's expression and stood to listen.

"You have been the greatest friend a person could ever have," Sadie said, hugging Bethany real tight.

"Sadie, why are you talking like this?" Bethany asked, frightened.

"I love you, Beth. I always will," Sadie said and started walking towards Zane.

"Sadie…wait," Bethany called, but Sadie didn't seem to hear.

"Come closer, chicken," Zane choked with anger. Seth remained where he was.

"Zane, give me the gun," Sadie said, stopping beside him.

"No!" Zane screamed, shoving Sadie aside as he stepped forward.

"Zane," Seth started. "I want you to know that I'm very sorry for what I've done to your family. Will you forgive me?"

"Never!" Zane screamed, pointing his gun at Seth's head. "On your knees!"

Seth obeyed and knelt where he was.

"Zane, don't do this," Sadie shouted, pulling on his arm that held his gun.

Zane again shoved Sadie aside and pointed his gun at Seth's head once more.

"Yurr gonna die, chicken," Zane hissed. "Suffer like we did."

Zane cocked his gun and aimed right between Seth's eyes.

"NO!!" Sadie screamed and ran in front of the gun.
BANG!

The gun fired and everyone gasped. Seth was still kneeling, but he wasn't dead like everyone had thought. Instead, he was weeping as he held the limp body of Sadie in his lap.

Zane sobered immediately. "Sadie?" he whispered. He dropped his gun like it was a disease and walked over to where Sadie lay. "Sadie?" he whispered once more as he knelt at her side.

Sadie breathed laboriously and opened her eyes to gaze upon her friends and family.

"Zane," she croaked.

"Here," he said, taking her cold hand in his.

"Forgive," she breathed. Her eyes closed slowly and everyone froze.

Seth felt for a pulse and found a faint one. "We need to get her to the doctor!"

Everyone scrambled to hitch the team on Mrs. Skinner's wagon and Zane gently picked up Sadie and laid her in the back. When the wagons were secure, they drove off as fast as they dared without hurting Sadie's chance for survival. Doc Brickner's was just behind the mercantile. They all prayed he wouldn't be out on a house call.

They reached town in fifteen minutes and as soon as they stopped, Zane checked Sadie's pulse and breathing. Bethany and Melody ran for the Doc.

"Doc Brickner!" Bethany called through his door while she and Melody pounded on it as hard as they could. They heard the lock unlatch so they quit pounding.

"What in tar nation…" Doc Brickner said as he opened the door.

"It's Sadie," Melody interrupted. "She's been shot."

"I'll get my bag," the Doc said, running up his stairs two at a time.

A small crowd began to gather. Amongst them was Sheriff Drake. Zane made sure he didn't make eye contact with him because he didn't want to give himself away; not just yet.

Doc examined Sadie's wound and checked her heart beat with his stethoscope. Sadie's eyes fluttered and opened, but she didn't seem to notice anyone.

"Zane," she called chokingly.

"Right here, sis," he said, holding her hand.

"Forgive…him," she croaked.

"I'll try, Sadie," he whispered.

She took two deep, jagged breaths and Zane shot a frightened look at the doc. The doc shook his head and hopped out of the back of the wagon, running up his stairs two at a time. Tears welled up in Zane's eyes. Had he killed his own sister? He gazed into Sadie's eyes. She looked up at him and smiled.

"I love…you…David." Sadie took a couple deep breaths. "Remember…Jesus." She closed her eyes for the last time.

"Sadie…no…don't leave me," Zane said, squeezing her hand.

"Remember," she breathed. Her hand went limp in Zane's and she stopped breathing.

"NO!!!" Zane screamed. "Sadie," he moaned. He then lay his head on her chest and wept with all his might. Seth sat there praying for the release of Zane's soul and Mrs. Skinner and the girls were now hugging each other and weeping.

After a few moments, Zane looked up at Seth. He stared at Seth for what seemed like an eternity. Zane noticed a flicker of something familiar in Seth's eyes.

REMEMBER ME, MY SON.

Zane's heart seemed to break into a thousand pieces. He suddenly felt all warm inside and for a moment, he thought it was the liquor in his system. But, as he continued to gaze into Seth's eyes, he realized it was the Holy Spirit taking hold of his soul. He laid Sadie's hand on her chest and hopped out of the back of the wagon.

"How did this happen, Zane?" the sheriff asked quietly.

Zane looked at Bethany and Melody and then back at Seth. Seth nodded so Zane looked at the sheriff.

"I did it," he said, pulling himself up to full height and taking a deep breath.

"Why?" the sheriff asked, unbelieving.

Zane went on to explain his pig-headedness and how Sadie came to be the victim rather than Seth.

"Well…" the sheriff was at a crossroads. He knew his duty was to arrest Zane, but he found himself questioning the law in this case for none of Sadie's friends wished to press charges against him.

"I guess you'll have to take me in now, Sheriff."

"Ahh, Zane," the sheriff moaned. "This is tough." He paused and thought for a moment.

"Aren't you gonna arrest me?" Zane asked.

The sheriff breathed a frustrated sigh and took Zane by the arm. "Let's go."

"Wait," Zane said, jumping up into the wagon once more. "Good bye, Sadie. I love you."

As he climbed out of the wagon, everyone gave him a hug.

"We'll come visit you, Zane," Bethany said quietly. "Be strong."

Seth watched as the sheriff led Zane through the crowd. His heart was broken, for he considered this to be partly his fault. If he hadn't committed his crime twelve years before, Sadie would still be alive and Zane wouldn't have to carry this guilt. He vowed to God and himself that he would go visit Zane that evening.

As the crowd dissipated, Bethany, Melody and Mrs. Skinner gathered around the wagon to look at Sadie's limp body.

"She looks so peaceful," Melody said, touching Sadie's hand.

"She's in Heaven now. We must remember that she gave her life for all of us." Mrs. Skinner took Bethany's and Melody's hands and led them to the garden behind the store. They sat on the bench and prayed and wept together.

Seth stood at the foot of the wagon and just stared at Sadie. He felt numb inside. Where was God's comfort in this? He wanted it to be all right and Sadie to be alive. It wouldn't be so. She was gone. She gave her life for his. *WHY!* his mind screamed at God.

MY SON.

Seth was knocked back into reality. He knew that the Lord was trying to get his attention. "Yes, Lord?" he whispered.

SHE'S WITH ME.

I know she's with you, Lord, he thought. *But we want her here. This shouldn't have happened.*

IT WAS FOR MY GLORY AND ZANE'S SALVATION THAT I ALLOWED IT, MY SON.

Seth couldn't listen anymore. He went inside the stock room at the mercantile and huddled in a corner. He wanted to curl up and die. He felt he was being consumed by guilt. All he could do was ask 'why'.

"It wasn't your fault, Seth," Bethany said quietly. "It was God's will."

Seth began to weep. He buried his face in his hands and wept like a little child. Bethany slowly walked over to where he was and encircled him like a mother would. Seth seemed to collapse in her arms as they both wept for the loss of their friend.

✡ ✡ ✡ ✡

Zane sat in his cell and just stared at the floor. He felt numb; and yet he was starting to understand why this all came about. He'd been going over the events of that day for hours trying to figure out the 'why's'. It was dark now and the Sheriff had locked up for the night and gone upstairs to bed.

As Zane sat in the deafening silence of night, there was a knock on the door.

"One moment," the sheriff called from his room above the jail. He came down the stairs, rubbing his eyes and trying to find the key. He looked through the peep hole on the door. "What is he doing here?" he whispered to himself. The sheriff unlocked the door and slowly swung it open. "Visiting hours are over, son," he said quietly.

"Could I please come in, Sheriff?" Seth pleaded. "I need to talk to Zane."

The sheriff looked over at Zane. Zane nodded and the sheriff let Seth in.

"Don't take too long. I'd like to get some shut eye." Sheriff Drake sat in his desk chair and kicked his feet up on his desk.

"Thank you, Sheriff." Seth walked slowly over to the cell. "Hello, Zane."

Zane didn't answer. He didn't know what to feel about this guy anymore.

"I have to ask you again," Seth started. "Will you forgive me? If I hadn't done what I did, you wouldn't be in this place…and your sister would still be…alive."

Zane looked long and hard at Seth. He remembered his sister's last words. Could he actually forgive him? He took a deep breath and sighed. "Seth," Zane started. "I've been a complete fool. I've wasted my whole life hating you when all I needed to do was forgive you and go on."

Zane thought of his sister. "She was so at peace," he sniffed. *"God, forgive me!"* he groaned. His lack of emotion now disturbed him; but he had spent all of it hours ago and was now simply drained and exhausted.

Seth grabbed the bars and then saw the keys hanging on the wall a few feet away. He quietly reached for them and unlocked the cell door. The sheriff had fallen asleep so he didn't know what was going on. Seth set the keys down and ran over to where Zane was slumped over. Zane grabbed onto Seth and hugged him so hard, Seth thought he wouldn't be able to breathe. They both stood there for a few minutes.

As they stepped away from each other, Zane took a couple deep breaths to try to calm himself.

"I'm sorry…Seth," Zane said chokingly.

"For what?" Seth asked in surprise.

"I'm sorry…for holding such anger and hate towards you for so many years. Do you forgive me?" Zane asked, staring at the ground.

"Of course I do." Seth stared at the ground. "Will you forgive me?"

Zane looked at Seth through new eyes; the eyes of mercy and grace. "Yes…I forgive you." Then he chuckled.

"What's so funny?" Seth asked.

"Don't tell anyone I hugged you, okay?" Zane said smiling.

Seth nodded and left.

✡ ✡ ✡ ✡

The next day, Sadie was buried in the plot right next to her parents. Almost everyone in town was at the service. All except Zane, who, of course, was still in jail. As the crowd dissipated, Bethany stayed behind to have a few moments alone.

"I'll miss you, Sadie," she whispered, wiping a lone tear from her cheek. "I wish things could've turned out different, but I know you're in a better place." She left the cemetery and rode out to Mrs. Skinner's where her friends were all meeting. They sat around the dining table with a Bible in the center until the wee hours of the morning. Some cried; some sat silently. All remembered that a dear friend had given her life for another.

EPILOGUE

ONE YEAR LATER

It was a warm, clear day in Pfeiffer's Landing. Besides a substantial line of gray far out over the western horizon, the sky was an opalescent blue. Flowers colored the hills and fields and the ocean roared its sweet, melancholy song. Bethany smiled as she saddled her horse; she loved days like this. She felt closer to the Lord somehow. Once her saddle was in place, she tied all of the roses she had cut from her rosebushes to the side of her saddlebags. She mounted the spirited mare and rode off toward town. As she'd planned no other task for the day than the one at hand, she took her time, reveling in the cool ocean breeze and the winsome voice of the gulls.

As Bethany reached town, she stopped by the mercantile for a few minutes. Mrs. Skinner was sweeping the porch. "Hello, Nanna," Bethany greeted.

"Hello, dear," Mrs. Skinner said, hugging Bethany like she was her own daughter.

"Is Seth here?" Bethany asked quietly.

"Yes. He's out back taking a break." Mrs. Skinner gazed into Bethany's eyes for a moment. "Is something wrong, dear?"

"No," Bethany said pensively. "It's been a year today since…"

"Oh." Mrs. Skinner smiled and gently stroked her cheek.

"I was just headed over to the cemetery." Bethany took a deep breath to calm her rapidly beating heart.

"Well, tell Seth that if he wants to go with you that I said it was fine." Mrs. Skinner felt compassion for them, but she didn't want to show pity. She, too, remembered the pain of that fateful day, but she wanted to be the strong one.

"Okay. Thank you," Bethany said, walking into the store. She looked around for Seth and her eye was caught momentarily by a beautiful dress in the back window. She walked out the back door and found Seth sitting by the rose garden, reading his Bible.

"Hi, honey," she greeted fondly.

"Beth," he chimed cheerfully. "To what do I owe this surprise?"

"Nanna said it would be okay if you wanted to join me… if you're up to it."

"Join you where?" he asked, a little confused.

"I'm going to the cemetery," she said, staring off into the distance. "I've brought roses."

"Ah," he said, "Of course, I'll join you." His tone became somber. "Just let me get my hat."

"Okay. I'll wait in the store." Bethany smiled faintly and turned to go inside. She decided to take a look at the dress she'd seen earlier. It was floor length with a double full skirt. It had full sleeves, cut short and a lace collar. But the best thing about it was the color. It was emerald green taffeta with a sea foam green satin sash. There were even shoes to match, which is the first time Bethany had seen anything like that.

"Beautiful, isn't it?" Seth said, coming up behind her.

"Yes, it is," Bethany replied, touching the fabric like it was fine china.

"It would look beautiful on you," he said, lightly stroking the back of her head. Seth loved Bethany's auburn curls.

"It would be a treat to have, but it's a little out of my price range," Bethany said, turning towards Seth. "Besides, I already have a green dress."

"Not like that one," Seth said, offering his arm as they were leaving the store.

"I'll bring him back real soon, Nanna," Bethany said, as they passed her on the porch.

"Take your time, kids. I'll be open 'till five tonight," Mrs. Skinner said, waving.

Seth and Bethany headed off toward the cemetery. It lay directly behind the church. They didn't say anything more to each other until they arrived.

"Do you want me to wait here?" Seth asked.

"Heavens, no," Bethany said, taking his hand. "You knew her longer than I did. You should be there."

They slowly walked to a beautiful spot under a willow located at the back end of the cemetery. There, under the willow, lay a simple marker with a name engraved next to a carving of a rose. It read, 'SADIE LYNN ALAN, born May, 1835 - died September, 1865'. *'Greater love hath no man than this; that he lay down his life for a friend'*. There was a rosebush growing next to the grave marker and there were numerous other bouquets left at the foot of the marker. Bethany bent down and picked up all the flowers that had wilted and threw them behind the tree. Then she carefully lay the roses she had brought in a nice arrangement on Sadie's grave.

"Hello, Sadie," Bethany said, forgetting Seth was there. "We miss you. Melody sends her best. The business is really growing now. I hope you don't mind, but I've re-opened your decorating service. We kept the name as a tribute to you. We know you would've wanted it to keep going." She slowly circled the marker, running her hand across the top of it. "Zane says he loves you and wishes he could be here. The Sheriff kept him from hanging for shooting you, but he couldn't keep Zane out of jail. It's good, though. He's witnessing to every prisoner that comes through there. He's even witnessing to the jailers. He told me to tell you that he no longer wants to be called Zane. He's ready to be called by his given name, David, now. He and Melody are planning on getting hitched when he gets out. I wish you could be here. Seth and I are getting married on Christmas Eve this year. It'll be a wonderful day, but I'll miss you terribly." Bethany smiled at Seth and stepped back a few steps.

Seth stepped up to the marker and placed a red rose on the top of it. "Hello, Sadie. We all miss you very much, but we're so grateful, especially me, for what you did. You gave your life for a friend and that's the highest, most loving thing you could do. Jesus did the same thing, you know." A lone tear trailed down his cheek. "I wish you could be here for the wedding. I would've loved to have you sing at the ceremony, but you're in a much better place then we could ever imagine. You're in the presence of our Lord. I'm jealous." He sniffed and smiled. "Well, we better be off. Rest easy, Sadie. We love you."

When Seth turned he saw Bethany standing by another marker a few yards away. He walked over to see who it was Bethany was visiting. When he arrived at her side, he noticed she was crying. "What's wrong, Beth?" he asked, slipping his arm around her shoulder.

"I miss my mamma," she whispered. "I wish she could be here to help me with the plans. I wish my father could be here to give me away."

Seth kissed her on the cheek and turned her toward him. "Are you having second thoughts?" he asked, looking intently into her emerald green eyes.

"No," she squeaked. "I just wish...oh, I know they're with God and all. I just miss them." She made a sweeping gesture to include Sadie.

"I know," Seth said, brushing the tears from her cheeks. "But, you have me."

Bethany blushed and smiled. "Yes...I do. I'm very grateful to the Lord that he brought you into my life on that magical day a year ago."

"I'm grateful He prompted me to settle here in Pfeiffer's Landing." Seth took her hand and led her back toward the horses. "Let's go."

"Okay," she said as they mounted their steeds. "I want to look at that dress again."

Seth smiled. "I thought you might."

In the Wake of Sorrow

In the wake of sorrow comes joy.
Tears which flow from a shattered heart
wash the wound.
Cries of grief reach His ear
and His blood flows;
Mingling with His own tears
His compassion falls.
Binding up with inexpressible love
every breach, every gap…
His radiant, swelling mercy
compassionately graces the deepest bruises
of our soul.
Beyond reason,
beyond measure;
nothing temporal, nothing eternal
can restrict or boundary the living,
healing embrace
of the Master's love.
When tears have flowed from a broken heart
oil and wine He pours;
healing every wound of the enemy's ploy;
in the wake of sorrow
comes joy.

Michael M. Middleton
*from *Sacred Journeys*

Made in the USA
Charleston, SC
18 August 2012